Praise for *The Rockford Files*

"Anyone watching *The Rockford Files* in the 1970s knew that it was a cut above. Even if, like me, you were just a kid being allowed to watch along with the adults, there was something about the show that made it stand out from the crowd of the other detective shows. In her terrific book, Amanda Keeler tells us why. Focusing on the producers' smart casting, playful genre mixing, and deft writing that could shift smoothly between car chases, comic banter, and socially relevant thematic concerns, Keeler reminds us why *The Rockford Files* was not just great entertainment but an important milestone in television history. This book is a joy to read."

—Jonathan Nichols-Pethick, author of *TV Cops: The Contemporary American Television Police Drama*

"Amanda Keeler has written an essential companion to *The Rockford Files*. Her book is brimming with enlightening insights and incisive commentary about this classic American detective drama."

—Michael Z. Newman, professor of English, University of Wisconsin–Milwaukee

"Amanda Keeler offers readers a sustained critical analysis of *The Rockford Files*, a popular and critically successful program both in its time and in syndication. This book fills a gap in the literature on popular television in the US, as there is very little critical or scholarly writing on *The Rockford Files*, despite the genre innovations it made and the warm place it continues to hold in the hearts of so many television viewers."

—Claudia Calhoun, professor, Hunter College, City University of New York

The Rockford Files

TV Milestones

Series Editor

Barry Keith Grant, Brock University

TV Milestones is part of the Contemporary Approaches to Film and Media Studies Series.

A complete listing of the books in this series can be found online at wsupress.wayne.edu.

The Rockford Files

Amanda Keeler

Wayne State University Press
Detroit

ISBN 9780814351000 (paperback)
ISBN 9780814351017 (ebook)

Library of Congress Control Number: 2025931233

On cover: 1978 Pontiac Firebird used in *The Rockford Files* and driven by James Garner. Courtesy of owner Cameron Jurd, Sydney, Australia. Used by permission.

Published with the assistance of a fund established by Thelma Gray James of Wayne State University for the publication of folklore and English studies.

Wayne State University Press rests on Waawiyaataanong, also referred to as Detroit, the ancestral and contemporary homeland of the Three Fires Confederacy. These sovereign lands were granted by the Ojibwe, Odawa, Potawatomi, and Wyandot Nations, in 1807, through the Treaty of Detroit. Wayne State University Press affirms Indigenous sovereignty and honors all tribes with a connection to Detroit. With our Native neighbors, the press works to advance educational equity and promote a better future for the earth and all people.

Wayne State University Press
Leonard N. Simons Building
4809 Woodward Avenue
Detroit, Michigan 48201-1309

Visit us online at wsupress.wayne.edu.

For my mom, who inspired and nurtured
my love of detective programs.
For my dad, who always has great stories to share
with me about music, movies, and television.

CONTENTS

Acknowledgments xi

Introduction: Creating Jim Rockford and *The Rockford Files* 1

1. "The Craziest Characters This Side of the Cuckoo's Nest" . . . 21

2. "Unlike Any Private Eye Series That Had Ever Been Done". . . 43

3. "The Stories Have Substance". 65

Conclusion: "He's Welcomed Back" 81

Notes 95

Works Cited 103

Index 109

ACKNOWLEDGMENTS

I am grateful to the Wayne State University Press TV Milestones editors Marie Sweetman and Barry Keith Grant, who helped guide this book project from the proposal to the final manuscript. I'm also thankful for the two peer-review readers, whose insights helped strengthen the book's argument and overall focus. Thank you to Seth Friedman for reading drafts, offering feedback, and reassuring me as I revised this manuscript.

Thanks as well to Valerie Beech, Marquette University librarian emerita, for helping me find archival materials related to the program. Thank you to Taylor Cole Miller for recommending digital resources. To Ruta Abolins, director, Brown Media Archives and Peabody Awards Collections at the University of Georgia, thank you for digitizing the four-part television news special *Violence in America* (1977).

I'm indebted to Ed Robertson and his book *45 Years of "The Rockford Files."* Robertson's book has been a tremendous resource, particularly his extensive interviews with the people who created, wrote, directed, produced, and starred on *The Rockford Files.*

For everyone whom I talked with about this book, who asked about its progress, and who encouraged me through revisions, thank you. For fellow fans of the show, your continued enthusiasm for *The*

Rockford Files, over fifty years after its premiere in 1974, gave me hope that there was an audience for this book. Thanks as well to Gigi Garner, who keeps her father James Garner's memory alive on social media, sharing stories of his life with his many fans.

As always, thanks to my husband, Daniel Murphy, for his endless patience with my research projects, graciously watching hour after hour of television with me, and encouraging me to occasionally leave the house to go for walks (and to beer gardens) with him.

INTRODUCTION

Creating Jim Rockford and *The Rockford Files*

What conventions and iconography would immediately connote a private detective on American television in the 1970s? Perhaps guns, binoculars, sketchy back alleys, or car chases? Each episode of *The Rockford Files* (1974–80) begins not with these images and situations, but those of boredom and restlessness: a half-finished solitaire game, half a cup of coffee, and an answering machine telling the viewer "this is Jim Rockford, please leave a message." The messages left by callers are sometimes about a late bill, a request to dog sit for the weekend, or a jacket lost by the dry cleaners. In quick succession the credits then present a montage, cutting from images of cars, highways, and the Hollywood sign, normally an image that evokes a world of glamour and celebrity culture. What follows is not a show about that world. These shots create an incongruity between the glitz of Southern California and the realities of nearly every aspect of the main character's life. Jim Rockford (James Garner) first appears on-screen driving his car and walking down a crowded sidewalk. In these shots viewers learn about Rockford's character, seemingly pensive and inquisitive, at work, watching, listening, and waiting. In one shot

Rockford is stationary on a sidewalk, appearing to linger while other pedestrians are blurred as they pass by, giving the effect of a man moving at his own pace while the world rushes around him. In the closing moments of the opening sequence a balance appears between Rockford at work and his leisure time, ending with several shots of him with his father, Joseph "Rocky" Rockford (Noah Beery Jr.), on the pier smiling, fishing, and just spending time together.

As much as these images speak to the complex character Jim Rockford, the music over the opening credits also creates an aural thematic space. Composed by Mike Post and Pete Carpenter, the program's theme song features "harmonica, synthesizer, electric guitar and driving percussion" that "merges associations of violence and sexuality with Rockford's country charm and straight-shooting character."[1] The Post-Carpenter score, combined with these specific instrument

Jim Rockford in the opening sequence of *The Rockford Files.*

choices, musically creates a bridge connecting the working-class guy to the big city private investigator.

This book focuses on how *The Rockford Files* reimagined the private detective television series, and how its creators took risks in crafting this historically important TV Milestone. The chapters that follow each explore how *The Rockford Files* stood out from a crowded landscape of private detective shows in the 1970s. Jon Abbott notes that "in a glut of prime-time cop and detective shows, *The Rockford Files* was unique for its time."[2] The much-loved program is considered to be "one of the finest private eye series of the 1970s, and indeed of all time" that resonated with audiences then and continues to be celebrated fifty years after its premiere.[3] Over its six seasons, from 1974 to 1980, the program's distinctive blend of elements, from the novelty of its characters, its experimentation with the private detective genre, its inclusion of women who wrote, produced, and directed the program, to its focus on contemporary social issues, define *The Rockford Files* as a TV Milestone.

But *The Rockford Files* was a show that almost wasn't a show. It might be considered a successful accident, one that only came about because of roadblocks within the television industry in the early 1970s.[4] Before co-creating *The Rockford Files*, Roy Huggins had been working for nearly two decades in television, writing for and creating several programs with characters inside or adjacent to police, private detectives, and the legal profession, such as *Maverick* (1957–62), *77 Sunset Strip* (1958–64), *The Fugitive* (1963–67), and *The Bold Ones: The Lawyers* (1969–72). Following in a similar narrative trajectory to his earlier work, Huggins had an idea for a new show and approached Stephen J. Cannell for his help in writing the script. At the time Cannell was working as a writer and producer on the television program *Toma* (1973–74). Huggins worked with Cannell to find a temporary replacement for *Toma*, whose production was running behind schedule due to the 1973 Writers Guild strike that had been settled several months prior. Huggins told Cannell the basic premise of his idea: "OK, this guy's name is Rockford, and he only handles closed cases. We'll call it *The Rockford Files*."[5] From there, Cannell set out to craft a private detective character unlike any other on television at the time. He recalled, "Nobody cared . . . what I was doing," so he took risks in creating Rockford's character by attempting to "break every cliché . . . in private eye fiction."[6] He was inspired by what he described as a "totally ludicrous" episode of another private detective drama, *Mannix* (1967–75), in which Joe Mannix (Mike Connors) agrees to work for a client who does not have the money to pay him.[7] In describing this new private detective character, Cannell shared an anecdote that summed up how Rockford would differ from Mannix. His new private detective would instead say, "Are you fucking kidding me? I've got overhead, I've got lights, I can't work for candy and quarters."[8] What resulted from Cannell's character experimentation was the inimitable creation of Jim Rockford, a lovable and relatable yet perpetually down-on-his-luck, pardoned ex-con and working-class private investigator. Each week the writers placed Rockford in a different case, all while surrounding him with a mélange of eclectic friends and family who helped (and sometimes hindered) his work.

Genre

It is important to begin by acknowledging that *The Rockford Files* was not a television program about the police. Creating the show around a private detective, rather than a police officer, allowed *The Rockford Files* to depict characters engaging in illegal activity in a way that police or detective programs could not. When it premiered in 1974, *The Rockford Files* was among several other programs on the air that featured private investigators, including *Mannix*, *Ironside* (1967–75), *Cannon* (1971–76), *Harry O* (1973–76), and *Barnaby Jones* (1973–80), as well as several that had recently ended: *Cool Million* (1972), *Banacek* (1972–74), *The Snoop Sisters* (1972–74), *Faraday & Company* (1973–74), and *Tenafly* (1973–74).

In this moment in the 1970s, *The Rockford Files* defined itself through genre hybridity. As David Thorburn describes it, *The Rockford Files* "is something of a hybrid, combining elements of comedy and the daytime continuing serial with the private eye format."[9] To set itself apart from its contemporaries, the program blended several existing and successful genres and storytelling modes together. Some critics recognized the program as borrowing elements from westerns, particularly ones that James Garner had previously starred on, such as *Nichols*. Rockford's character is in some ways an update to the character Bret Maverick from *Maverick*, a kind man and expert gambler, who was also a "drifter who often ran afoul" of the existing power structures in the towns he visited.[10] As Dahlia Schweitzer writes, "Clearly, Huggins felt that the best way to modernize a western hero was to make him a private detective, thus reinforcing the notion of the private eye as the natural successor to the cowboy."[11]

The program's overall attitude toward crime challenged the "law and order," ideologically conservative nature of many police/detective dramas of the 1960s and 1970s, on which police officers are portrayed as uncomplicated, noble heroes—as good guys (mostly white men) who fearlessly restore order while saving those in peril, such as *The F.B.I.* (1965–74), the 1960s return of *Dragnet* (1967–70), *Adam-12* (1968–75), and *Hawaii Five-O* (1968–80). As Jonathan Nichols-Pethick writes, many critics of police dramas view them as television programs following a "formula" that "provides moral reassurance and champions an inherently conservative social agenda by focusing on the essential wisdom and virtue of those who enforce the law (police officers, district attorneys, etc.) and offer protection from all who threaten the social order."[12] Similarly, Roger Sabin writes that "cop dramas often address fears expressed by communities in the face of perceived increases in crime rates, in a dual effort to provoke anxiety as well as reassure."[13] While many 1970s police dramas align with Nichols-Pethick's and Sabin's assessments, *The Rockford Files* takes this formula and nearly completely subverts it, questioning the wisdom of police authorities, actively interrogating the established social order—essentially asking viewers to examine and to think about the world of this television program, but also about how it connects to the real world.

Media critics such as Allen Barra note how *The Rockford Files* channeled Raymond Chandler "updated to the 1970's."[14] Mark Alvey assesses that the show was a "revisionist take on the hard-boiled detective genre."[15] Though described by David Marc as a "kind of post-nuclear Sam Spade," Rockford does not neatly fit into the category of the hard-boiled, loner main characters of literature and film during the 1930s–40s.[16] *The Rockford Files* isn't set in the bleak, black-and-white landscape of *Double Indemnity* (Billy Wilder, 1944) or *The Big Sleep* (Howard Hawks, 1946), nor the dusty western towns of *Maverick*. Part of *The Rockford Files*'s revision and innovation of the genre involved creating a particular visual and aural style for the show, set in the highly recognizable geography of the greater metropolitan area of Los Angeles, but not the well-known tourist spaces. Instead, the locations focus on the everyday, banal spaces of bland office buildings, nondescript apartments, seedy bars, and dimly lit restaurants that worked to create scenarios in which crime, corruption, and malfeasance exist in plain sight. The images of a busy and chaotic city do define the spaces of the show, though his investigations just as often take Rockford to small towns and rural, two-lane highways. The constant change of setting reinforces the chaotic nature of his investigations and his nomadic existence.

The success of *The Rockford Files* is also rooted in its main character, Jim Rockford. Much of the writing on the program celebrates the distinctiveness and complexity of Rockford's character, the "ordinary guy as detective," and how he defied the conventional "tough guy" persona prevalent across police and detective dramas.[17]

Who Is Jim Rockford?

The quirky intricacies of Jim Rockford's character are at the center of what makes *The Rockford Files* remarkable. Rockford's character, at its heart, is defined by a complex series of contradictions that make him multifaceted and somewhat unpredictable. David Thorburn describes Rockford as an "unpretentious and decent" private detective who was more often "nursing his own injuries than inflicting them on others."[18] He's a working-class private investigator who fits in easily among most people, though he seems to scoff somewhat when interacting with wealthy people while on a case, such as at a party in "The Countess" (September 27, 1974). Rockford fits within traditional modes of masculinity—strong, tall, deep voiced, charming, and physically foreboding, with a take-charge demeanor. Yet, he is also a coward. As Bill Carter notes, at his core Rockford is someone "who would rather crack wise than fight," demonstrated, for example, in "Profit and Loss, Part 1: Profit" (December 20, 1974) when a character tells Rockford, "I was told you were really reliable," to which he answers, "Reliable but chicken."[19]

Rockford is highly intelligent, and an effective private investigator. He deftly uncovers the root causes of his clients' troubles, though these cases often lead to car chases and fistfights. He is knowledgeable about the law and proper procedures, even when he chooses not to follow them. Rockford generally knows a lot about the things he encounters every day, such as his bullet expertise in "The Four Pound Brick" (February 21, 1975). In this episode, Rockford is investigating the alleged accidental death of a police officer. He dismantles a live cartridge, looking to see if it is a "light load" like the Los Angeles Police Department uses. Despite his investigative acumen and knowledge base, Rockford is barely scraping by financially because his clients find multiple ways to avoid paying him, such as in "Find Me If You Can" (November 1, 1974) when his client Barbara Kelbaker (Joan Van Ark) does not have the money to pay him because she wants to

Rockford's loyal companion, his Pontiac Firebird.

return the money she stole, or in "The Four Pound Brick" when Rocky and Kate (Edith Atwater) both want to pay Rockford's bill, but both tell him in private that they are a little short on cash and won't be able to pay right now.

Overall, *The Rockford Files* "is the story of a man who wants to be left alone, but whose lot in life is never to be."[20] As Garner says about the character, "Rockford has no ambition beyond being able to pay his bills, go fishing with his dad, and drink a few beers while watching football on TV."[21] He lives alone in his trailer on the beach, which serves as both his home and his office. Rockford is mostly an honest person, though he isn't afraid to bend the law or dabble in playful deceit to advance his investigative work. Many episodes of the show feature Rockford bending and breaking the law in order to move forward with his investigations. Rockford is, as Geoff Tibballs describes the character,

Rockford's trailer, his Pontiac Firebird, and Rocky's truck in "The Attractive Nuisance" (January 6, 1978).

a "kindly con-man."[22] Garner notes in an interview "you know, he's tricky. He's very tricky. But he wasn't *bad*."[23] He lies when necessary; in "The Countess" he tells Lieutenant Alex Diel (Tom Atkins) that he was meeting with Carl Brego (Dick Gautier) about Brego hiring him, when he was actually there telling him to stop blackmailing Deborah Ryder (Susan Strasberg).

While not the subject of every episode, at its core *The Rockford Files* is about a man attempting to live his life after being wrongfully convicted and serving five years in prison and later released with a full pardon from the governor. Though pardoned, Rockford is marked by his conviction and time in prison, forever labeled an untrustworthy felon by the police. Rockford's very existence is defined by this ongoing psychic trauma, and it manifests in his everyday struggle to move ahead in life after his wrongful conviction. This injustice defines his investigative work and the types of clients that seek him out for help. In critic Robert Lloyd's assessment, "Rockford is not interested in the law, but in justice," a narrative focus that differed greatly from other competing series in the 1970s.[24] Rockford used his misfortunes to form his underlying purpose and mission, to bring a modicum of justice in a world he sees as overwhelmed with injustices.

Through the series Rockford has a complicated relationship with law enforcement. He has a friend on the police force, Dennis Becker (Joe Santos), a Los Angeles police detective who begrudgingly helps Rockford with small favors, such as giving him the name connected to a license plate or running fingerprints. As James Lardner notes, Dennis "is continually called upon to perform special favors for Rockford to the detriment of his police career."[25] Dennis and Rockford have a symbiotic relationship, though their friendship at times creates tension in both men's lives and careers, such as in "The Mayor's Committee from Deer Lick Falls" (November 25, 1977), when Dennis is chastised by his boss after Rockford files a police report connected to one of his private detective cases. While his relationship with Dennis aligns Rockford somewhat with official law enforcement, Police Lieutenants Alex Diel and Doug Chapman (James Luisi) repeatedly suspect Rockford of committing felonies even though he is innocent, such as in "The Battle of Canoga Park" (September 30, 1977) when it is proven that Rockford's gun was stolen and used by another person to commit a murder. Diel and Chapman do not professionally recognize Rockford as an equal and generally refuse to work with him even when he presents them with evidence of the illegal activities happening on their watch. Some of this reluctance to cooperate with Rockford stems from their fear that he will solve cases that the police cannot. In his memoir James Garner writes, "The top brass can't stand Rockford because he makes them look bad by solving cases."[26] This is perhaps a class and professional issue too—Rockford the ex-con, barely scraping by financially, regularly does better at investigations than the trained and more highly compensated police officers.

Though living alone, Rockford was not a loner. According to Cannell, since "private eyes never have family" he created Rockford's father, Rocky, to break from the usual depiction of private detectives as solitary characters.[27] Rocky, a retired trucker, frequently tells Rockford how much he disapproves of his work as a detective, but Rockford seems to enjoy it most of the time—why else would he continue to do a thing that does not pay well and that frequently gets him beaten up? Rocky, a "genial, folksy father," is the ideal counterbalance to Rockford's outlandish pursuits.[28] Besides his father, Rockford has a group of friends who seem to need his help constantly, which I discuss in detail in chapter one. He would do anything for these friends, even when it means putting himself in danger. Rockford's entire existence is built on his status as a man who is underappreciated and whose expertise is frequently ignored, who has nonetheless dedicated his professional life to fighting for others in the same position, a Robin Hood–esque existence with limited financial success. Rockford is drawn to injustices in the world and makes it his job to fight against them. This blend of character traits, at once a private detective able to solve difficult cases, and yet also unable to function within the same parameters as his friends and family, demonstrates a complexity of character crafted by this TV Milestone's talented writing staff, which I discuss in chapter two.

The steadiest things in Rockford's life are his trailer and his car, the Pontiac Firebird, but these are not safe spaces. He is constantly in peril in them, between people breaking in to his trailer or attempting to blow it up, such as in "The Battle of Canoga Park," or people cutting his brake lines in order to cause bodily harm to throw him off a case. The frequent use of his car acknowledges the large geographic area covered in his investigations and allowed for numerous car-focused action sequences. It also represented one interpretation of Rockford's prowess. As Richard Meyers writes, driving was "the only thing Rockford was really good at."[29]

The critical celebrations of Rockford's character owe much to James Garner's acting abilities. Garner excelled at his portrayal of Jim

Rockford, but this was not his first television role. By the time that *The Rockford Files* aired, he had been working in film and television for two decades. In the 1950s he appeared on multiple episodes of *Cheyenne* (1955–63) and *Conflict* (1956–57), before starring on *Maverick* as the main character Bret Maverick. After *Maverick*, Garner starred in several well-regarded films, *The Children's Hour* (1961) with Audrey Hepburn, *The Great Escape* (1963) with Steve McQueen, *The Americanization of Emily* (1964) with Julie Andrews, and *Marlowe* (1969) with Rita Moreno and Bruce Lee. In the early 1970s he returned to television in *Nichols* (1971–72), a short-lived western series on NBC whose characters and storylines were similar to what would later appear on *The Rockford Files*.

The Rockford Files exuded a multifaceted tone, at times serious but also infused with humorous dialogue and character interactions. Part of Garner's charm on *The Rockford Files* was portraying Rockford inventing and playing new characters whenever it was necessary to elicit information for his investigations, such as in "Resurrection in Black & White" (November 7, 1975) when he pretends to be a real-estate broker (using his homemade business card machine in his car) or in "The Deep Blue Sleep" (October 10, 1975) when he "borrows" a police car and uses the police radio to call for backup to help save his client's life.

The program also played to James Garner's "comic gifts."[30] Ed Robertson notes that Garner created "a subtle, wry, understated humor that was based on a total understanding of the character's thoughts and motivations."[31] In a 1979 *Esquire* profile of Garner, Jean Vallely writes that "very few actors can do what Garner does," in that Garner was able to effortlessly embody a complex character and perform both comedic and dramatic moments, sometimes seconds apart.[32] Tom Shales suggests that *The Rockford Files* was "funnier than many comedies."[33] For John Leonard, the program worked by "combining the wit of the best sitcoms with the pace and action and relentless camera-work of the best cop shows."[34]

In terms of his six-year run playing Rockford, as Jon Abbott notes, Garner "invested . . . a world-weary cynicism and pessimism, a satisfying multi-dimensional and sympathetic portrayal."[35] For Bill Carter, Rockford represented a shift toward depictions of "more realistic heroes," imperfect, somewhat contradictory, but also charming and likeable.[36] James Garner claimed to like Rockford's character because he was "not a hero."[37] Garner noted in an interview that Rockford was "somebody who is likeable and yet, you know, strong, and not always perfect, not always right. I think people like to see that fallibility."[38] Garner writes in his memoir that "every real private detective I've ever talked to said Rockford was much closer to the truth than a lot of the tough ones on the screen."[39] Yet, Rockford's actual existence, his life and his work, is (hopefully) not realism, not a reality lived by any real person, and not to be envied.

Television critics were impressed with Garner's portrayal of Rockford, even after the program had been on the air for multiple seasons. As Gail Williams noted in *The Hollywood Reporter* in 1979, "James Garner's panache as private eye Jim Rockford hasn't dimmed a bit in six years, and he still has the cleverest comebacks and insults in town."[40] While still intact and long ingrained by the sixth season of the program, these character traits written by Cannell and brought to life by Garner were evident from the very beginning of the series.

Series Premiere: "I Get Kidnapped by Two Guys and They Beat the Poo out of Me"[41]

Before NBC executives ordered *The Rockford Files* as a series, it premiered as a movie of the week on Wednesday, March 27, 1974.[42] NBC picked up the show as a series for its fall schedule and premiered the program on September 13, 1974. "The Kirkoff Case" begins with Rockford trailing someone in his car, presumably working on a case. He follows this car to the beach where he meets Tawnia Baker (Julie Sommars), and after some snarky banter, she invites him over to her apartment for a drink. There, she drugs Rockford, and he passes out in the hallway of her apartment building, waking up later in her apartment with a gun in his face. Travis Buckman (Roger Davis) asks Rockford whom he is working for, and though he says that it is confidential, a wave of the gun immediately persuades Rockford to tell him the answer, Larry Kirkoff (James Woods). Rockford, always hoping to avoid injury and violence, first demonstrates this character trait here.

The original and distinctive premise of *The Rockford Files* was that Rockford would only work on closed cases, which is the status of the investigation he is working on in this episode. Here, he is looking into the unsolved murders of Mr. and Mrs. Kirkoff after the police stopped investigating because they failed to prove Larry Kirkoff killed his parents. Larry Kirkoff offers Rockford $20,000 to solve his parents' murders. Later, Rockford returns to his trailer where his father, Rocky, is waiting with several telephone messages. A woman called but didn't

Rockford works with Larry Kirkoff to solve two murder cases.

leave her name, and Rocky tells Rockford that "they're getting mighty smart, those bill collectors," cleverly insinuating that Rockford is a man that owes people money, and that this might be a chronic condition for him. Rockford goes to meet this woman, and when he gives his car to the valet, several men beat him up and drive him to an empty warehouse, where they knock out one of his teeth. In an attempt to avoid additional bodily harm, Rockford tells Muzzy (Philip Kenneally) whatever he wants to hear so Muzzy's men will stop punching him. Rockford goes to the police, specifically Dennis Becker, to report the assault, and Dennis is gruff and tells Rockford that "every time you come in here with a bloody nose morale goes up 10 points," establishing their complicated friendship. While investigating who owns the condemned warehouse where he was assaulted, Rockford ends up in a high-speed car chase in his ever-present Pontiac Firebird. Rockford eventually figures out that Muzzy was hired by Mr. Kirkoff to kill Mrs. Kirkoff, but that Mr. Kirkoff's son Larry killed his father. Rockford attempts to collect the $20,000 Larry promised him but is scared off by Larry's dog. Rockford convinces Tawnia to pursue the case against Larry for murdering his father. He tells Tawnia his fee, $200 a day plus expenses, the amount he charges that would remain steady throughout the series. They soon find out that Larry confessed to the killing, so she immediately fires Rockford.

Rockford demonstrates a keen sense of reading people, holding his own even when he encounters other smart people. He successfully solves the case but is not paid for his efforts. He is beaten up and loses a tooth, and flinches at guns and dogs, but manages to make it out of the investigation mostly unscathed. By the end of the first episode of the series, it is clear how the program is blending the conventional with the unconventional, mixing some existing expectations of the police and private detective genre with novel character traits and situations as it seeks to stake out new narrative territory.

The critical reviews of this premiere episode were mixed—*Variety*'s Bill Greeley praised James Garner's performance, writing that "the

Garner personality and mixture of humor with the potboiler elements give it a chance."[43] Though the show set out to innovate the genre, not all critics viewed it through this lens. John J. O'Connor's review describes what worked and what did not: "Mr. Garner's sardonic zaniness can be attractive. In his first episode he is very funny when the routines work, which unfortunately is only about half the time."[44] Gary Deeb notes that *The Rockford Files* "is just another detective show, with Jim as a gumshoe who handles only the tough ones," but did single out the show's star for praise: "As always, Garner is humorous, laconic, and lightly romantic."[45]

Despite these mixed reviews, the show scored highly in the national Nielsen ratings. "The Kirkoff Case" ranked as the twenty-first most watched program the week it aired in September 1974, rising to nineteenth for the series' sixth episode, "This Case Is Closed" (October 18, 1974), and to the tenth most watched program with "Caledonia—It's Worth a Fortune!," which aired on December 6, 1974.[46] The program remained well regarded by viewers and critics during its six-year run, though it did not appear again in the top-twenty rated programs after its first year on air. In December 1979 Gary Deeb ran a poll about television programs that received "more than 55,000 responses from TV watchers, who were invited to name their favorite programs on each night."[47] *The Rockford Files* was the viewer favorite for Friday nights, with 2,316 votes, more than double the number of votes for the second-place program *Dallas* (910 votes). Deeb, though initially unimpressed with the show, does by 1979 concede that *The Rockford Files* is "the only Friday program with a shred of intelligence."[48]

Overall, *The Rockford Files* was not only watched each week by millions of viewers, but it also caught the attention of several major awards organizations, including the Emmy Awards, the Golden Globes, the Grammys, and the Writers Guild. In total, the program was nominated for seventeen Emmy Awards, with five wins, including the 1978 Outstanding Drama Series. For performances, James Garner won an Emmy for Outstanding Lead Actor in a Drama Series in

1977, and Stuart Margolin won two Emmy Awards—Outstanding Continuing Performance by a Supporting Actor in a Drama Series in 1979 and Outstanding Supporting Actor in a Drama Series in 1980—for his portrayal of Rockford's friend/foe Angel Martin. *The Rockford Files* also received four Golden Globe nominations, three of which were for James Garner for Best TV Actor, and one for Best TV Series in 1980. In 1978 James Garner won a People's Choice Award for Favorite Male TV Performer. Composers Mike Post and Pete Carpenter also won the 1975 Grammy for Best Instrumental Arrangement for their contributions to *The Rockford Files*. Juanita Bartlett was nominated for a Writers Guild of America Award for Television: Episodic Drama for the episode "So Help Me God" (November 19, 1976). Many years after the show stopped airing new episodes, the now defunct cable channel Sleuth ran an online poll in 2006 that ranked Jim Rockford as the third best of "America's Top Sleuths," behind Lieutenant Columbo (Peter Falk) and Thomas Magnum (Tom Selleck) from *Magnum, P.I.*[49]

While it is clear from these reviews, awards, and Nielsen ratings that the television program was widely viewed by audiences, the makeup of its audience is less clear. According to Amanda D. Lotz, "the critically acclaimed *Rockford Files* was arguably the creative pinnacle" of NBC's schedule in the mid-1970s, yet at the time NBC was in last place in terms of the popularity of its programs, and the number of its programs in the top twenty in terms of ratings.[50] Television critic Les Brown noted in 1977 that *The Rockford Files* "appeal[ed] in the main to older viewers."[51] This changed in 1978–79, according to Ed Robertson, who noted that "the series was becoming increasingly popular among young adults" once it started airing on "late night reruns."[52]

There was one aspect of *The Rockford Files*'s reputation that hinted at the possibility that the show also attracted younger viewers. The program was frequently denounced as overly violent, deemed so by the National Parent Teacher Association (PTA), which found the program to be "objectionable because of gratuitous violence."[53] In 1979 the PTA labeled the program a "time waster."[54] In 1981, *The New*

York Times published an article—"Lawyer Says 9-Year-Old Bank Robber Was Influenced by TV Crime"—and noted that "the day before the robbery" the alleged bank robber "had spent hours watching" *The Rockford Files*, as well as several other television programs.[55] While anecdotal, this newspaper article does suggest that the program did attract younger viewers, who by 1981 would have been watching reruns of the show in syndication.[56] In retrospect the show does not seem so violent as to warrant the PTA warning labels, and its use of violence was largely relegated to fistfights and car chases. James Garner noted that "we weren't allowed to do a lot of gunfire and that sort of thing. Network wouldn't allow it . . . so, our car action was our action. That and a few fistfights here and there. But not many gunfights."[57] Executive Producer Meta Rosenberg made an important distinction about the violence that does appear on *The Rockford Files*: "The show has never been based on violence, but at least the violence we have is real. When someone gets hit, they hurt."[58] As co-creator Stephen J. Cannell noted in 1977, "there is incredible pressure on right now to eliminate violence from scripts."[59] Nonetheless, the amount of violence depicted on the program changed little over its six seasons, so it is unclear how much the pressure on writers was reflected in the episodes that aired.

In this TV Milestones book I focus on the aspects of *The Rockford Files* that have not been discussed as much in the existing scholarship. Even with the many books and articles about the show, there is still much to be said about this tremendously influential and entertaining television program, particularly because its reputation continues to flourish even after fifty years. Many writers commented about how the show never truly stopped airing as Universal was "aggressive about getting the show into syndication" where it became a "staple of afternoon and late-night programming throughout the '80s."[60] *The Rockford Files*'s presence continues with the release of season DVDs and series box sets, and on streaming services like Philo and the Roku Channel.

The chapters that follow each explore innovative elements of *The Rockford Files*. In chapter one I discuss the multifaceted, eclectic characters and the actors and actresses who played these characters, and how those portrayals were central to the show's appeal to viewers and critics alike. This chapter examines Rockford's dad, Rocky; his attorney and on-again, off-again girlfriend Beth Davenport (Gretchen Corbett); his friend on the police force Dennis Becker; and Rockford's friend from prison, Angel Martin. The skill of the performers and their chemistry on-screen, combined with the writers' vision for these eccentric characters, produced an undeniably charming family that was uncommon on television at the time.

The show's creators and writers were responsible for crafting the complicated situations in which Rockford finds himself week after week. Chapter two examines writer Juanita Bartlett and director Meta Rosenberg, two women with extensive creative control working at a time when female writers, producers, and directors were overlooked and underutilized.[61] This chapter also examines Stephen J. Cannell as the co-creator of the series, producer and writer David Chase, and producer Charles "Chas." Floyd Johnson, and how each left their individual authorial mark on *The Rockford Files*.

Chapter three focuses on the subtle and not-so-subtle ways that the writers of *The Rockford Files* showcased social issues unconventionally throughout the run of the show. While the television program was considered by some to be a "light-weight" detective program, it did tackle some serious contemporary issues.[62] In the context of his private investigation business Rockford uncovered issues with the criminal justice system, grand juries, organized crime, elder abuse, real-estate fraud, and the increasingly intrusive uses of surveillance technologies. The program also touches on the psychic trauma and the miscarriage of justice of Rockford's wrongful conviction, and his everyday struggle to move ahead in life after serving time in prison. In line with other appealing aspects of *The Rockford Files*, the show's writers were able to entertain while also educating viewers about social issues and critiquing powerful people and institutions.

In the conclusion I discuss *The Rockford Files* made-for-television reunion movies that aired between 1994 and 1999, and how they revisited many themes and ideas present in the original series. After the made-for-television movies, there were unsuccessful attempts to reboot the show and to create a movie version of it in the 2010s. Though these re-envisioned versions of *The Rockford Files* fizzled, the program's legacy and essence continue to resonate through subsequent private detective programs. The show's ongoing relevance, now fifty years later, and its continued popularity speak to the chemistry, the creativity, and the timing that brought together the show's writers, directors, and performers to create this award-winning, genre-bending private detective program.

1

"THE CRAZIEST CHARACTERS THIS SIDE OF THE CUCKOO'S NEST"

The creators of *The Rockford Files* attempted to rethink the private-investigator character by playing around with the parameters of the genre set by many of the show's contemporaries.[1] Stephen J. Cannell's experiments with the private-detective genre were rooted, first and foremost, in his attempt to "break every cliché" in his creation of Jim Rockford, and continuing this experimentation with Rockford's friends and family.[2] As Mark Alvey notes, *The Rockford Files*'s strength was in its "fully-developed characters and richly-drawn relationships."[3] The show's distinctive cast of characters comes to life through the performances of, and the chemistry between, the actors and actresses involved in the show. In an interview included in the DVD box set of *The Rockford Files*, James Garner notes, "The secret to all of it, and I'll say it probably more than once, is writing. . . . He had good friends. He had his dad. . . . That's what makes up the nucleus of a series. . . . One guy can't do it. You gotta have all those people together."[4] Though the focus of the show is on Rockford's investigative work, the program also explored his family life and his friendships, allowing many characters the narrative space to explore their past and present lives and motivations.

As noted in the introduction, Rockford's core group includes his father, Rocky. The two spend a considerable amount of time together, fishing, cooking, swapping favors, and driving each other around town. In addition to his relationship with Rocky, Rockford's friend group consists of three regularly recurring characters. Beth Davenport is Rockford's attorney, friend, and sometimes romantic partner who frequently rescues him from his many legal troubles. Rockford also spends considerable time with his friend Dennis Becker, a Los Angeles police detective, whose complex friendship with Rockford shifts over the seasons, from sometimes helpful, to outwardly hostile, and then back again. Finally, many of Rockford's day-to-day frustrations come from his relationship with his friend from prison, Angel Martin, the endlessly needy, largely unsuccessful con artist that Rockford occasionally employs (quickly regretting it). Together, this motley group, deemed "the craziest characters this side of the cuckoo's nest," was instrumental to the charm and appeal of *The Rockford Files*.[5]

Joseph "Rocky" Rockford

Part of the success of *The Rockford Files* comes from the screen chemistry between James Garner and the show's ensemble members. In particular, Garner and Noah Beery Jr. craft a warmth together, producing a complex and relatable father-son relationship. As Garner writes in his memoir, "Rockford's relationship with his father is the emotional backbone of the show. Sometimes they get on each other's nerves, but the affection is there through it all."[6] Rocky's presence on the show came from Cannell's desire to revamp the private detective genre in multiple ways, first by giving Rockford a father. Cannell notes, "Private eyes never have family, so I gave him Joseph Rockford, his dad, who was a real blue-collar guy who drove a truck and was really embarrassed telling his buddies at the truck stop what Jimmy did for a living. And I basically wrote my relationship with my father, who was my greatest hero and my best friend, but who thought I was literally out of my mind trying to be a Hollywood writer."[7] Cannell used

Portrait of Rocky on Rockford's desk from the opening sequence.

his relationship with his father to construct the bond between Rockford and Rocky. The terrific chemistry created between Garner and Beery almost didn't happen. In the March 1974 made-for-television movie that launched the series, Rockford's father was played by Robert Donley.

As I noted in the introduction, Rocky's presence in Rockford's life is explicit from the opening credits, which depict father and son sharing time together fishing and laughing. In many ways, the writers situate their relationship by having Rocky just pop up even when he is not integral to the scene. Rockford's dad leads a pretty simple life, which the viewer learns from watching his interactions with Rockford and hearing about his past. Rocky has retired from trucking, and he has enough money to own his small house and his pickup truck, and to bail Rockford out after his many arrests, such as in the episode

"Piece Work" (December 17, 1976). Most of Rocky's days are spent fishing, hanging out with his friends, and helping Rockford with everyday errands and chores. Though they both seem to get annoyed with one another over little things, their relationship is reciprocal, always helping each other whenever the need arises, such as when Rocky needs help with his friend T. T. in "The Trees, the Bees and T. T. Flowers" (Parts 1 and 2, January 21 and 28, 1977), and vice versa, when Rockford needs Rocky to tow his trailer, which happens in "The House on Willis Avenue" (February 24, 1978). Rocky clearly loves his son but nonetheless has deep concerns about the line of work Rockford has chosen, even though Rockford is quite effective at solving cases for his clients. He really wants Rockford to leave the private detective business and become a trucker, which Rocky feels would be a much more respectable way to earn a living. He expresses these thoughts frequently, such as in the season one episode "This Case Is Closed" (October 18, 1974). Rocky tells Rockford, "You got to get yourself an office job like, you know, at least till you stop bleeding internally," which is both a push for Rockford to get out of the private detective business and a jab at how often Rockford finds himself bruised and injured because of his line of work.[8] In "The Mayor's Committee from Deer Lick Falls" (November 25, 1977) Rocky tells Rockford that an insurance company needs an investigator, something he deems safer and more respectable than being a private detective. Rocky's distaste for Rockford's profession even propels him to lie to his friends about what his son does for a living. In "The Four Pound Brick" (February 21, 1975) Rocky tells his friend Kate Banning that Rockford is a truck driver, but when business is slow "he's got himself sort of a sideline. . . . He's a private investigator." Of course, one of the reasons Rockford is an underpaid private investigator is because Rocky sometimes tells his friends that Rockford will do the work for free, as he does here with Kate.

While their love for one another comes across through the storylines, Rocky does find ways to praise other people's careers at the expense of Rockford's feelings, such as in "The Aaron Ironwood School

Rockford and Rocky in "Trouble in Chapter 17" (September 23, 1977).

of Success" (September 12, 1975). Rocky is embarrassed when Rockford comes to his house to pick him up in a borrowed pizza delivery car. The two men are about to go to the airport to pick up Aaron (James Hampton), a foster child that lived with them many years ago. During their ride to the airport, Rocky reminisces about what a great kid Aaron was and insinuates his disappointment that Rockford has not turned out more like Aaron. As they argue in the car, Rockford tells him that "I'm not exactly a failure either." Rocky says that he's sorry and that he is proud of Rockford and loves him, and yet "I just wish you'd worn a tie, that's all." Aaron tells Rockford that he approves of his work as a private detective, which causes Rocky to remark, "Why didn't you say so?" This interchange frees Rocky to be less ashamed of Rockford's professional choices, at least temporarily. In the end it is revealed that Aaron's success is not due to his business acumen, but rather a pyramid scheme he created to sell illegal franchises of his company. Even though Rocky views Aaron as more successful than his son, Rockford ultimately saves both of their lives before Aaron is arrested for fraud.

The season five episode "A Good Clean Bust with Sequel Rights" (November 3, 1978) highlights that while Rocky doesn't always understand Rockford's work, he nonetheless tries to find ways to connect with him. In this episode Rocky expresses his love for a detective television show, *Falcone*, especially its lead character's catch phrase: "Freeze turkey!" Rockford has been hired to "babysit" the man the character is based on, Frank Falcone (Hector Elizondo), and to keep him from getting into trouble during a press weekend "to keep the name and legend clean" for the launch of Falcone's toy line. Rockford tries his best to humor his father's love of this television program yet is confused about how Rocky does not respect Rockford's private detective work, even though both Falcone's character and Rockford work in similar professions.

There are times when Rocky treats Rockford's profession with respect, mostly when he needs Rockford to investigate things for him or his friends. In "The Four Pound Brick" Rocky even tells Rockford, "You know, I never did think much of this P.I. business. . . . Then this morning, I started seeing things in a different light, a whole different light." In this episode Rocky decides he needs Rockford's help in finding out if a friend's son was killed in an accident or was murdered.

In a complex, two-part episode told in flashbacks, "The Trees, the Bees and T. T. Flowers," Rocky desperately wants to help his friend T. T. (Strother Martin), who has been caught up, via his daughter Cathy (Karen Machon) and son-in-law Sherman (Alex Rocco), in a real-estate scheme to defraud T. T. of his land. Over the course of these two episodes, Rockford uncovers an elaborate scam, perpetrated by Sherman, who plans to sell T. T.'s valuable land to a real-estate developer. Rockford is forced to pretend to be dead in order to investigate the depths of this multilayered fraud. These episodes also highlight how the show used Rockford's cases to dramatize real-world issues such as real-estate fraud, which I discuss in chapter three.

The times when Rockford and Rocky try to connect the most are when their relationship tends to fall apart. In one of the last episodes of the series, "The Hawaiian Headache" (November 23, 1979), Rockford and Rocky win a trip to Hawaii, and they are hoping to have time to relax together and go fishing. The free trip ends up being a ruse orchestrated by Rockford's old Korean War sergeant, Colonel John Smith (Ken Swofford), who wants Rockford to go undercover for a money exchange mission. Rockford gets shot in the shoulder and then accused of murder; all the while Rocky feels abandoned and grows angrier with every passing minute. Eventually Rockford is able to help Smith with his case, but Rockford's vacation with Rocky is cut short, and they do not have the time to relax or go fishing. Being near the end of the series, an episode dedicated to Rocky being angry with Rockford isn't ideal. However, the next episode, "No Fault Affair" (November 30, 1979), which I discuss in chapter two, demonstrates a more fitting conclusion to the father-son relationship, ending with all of Rockford's closest friends hanging out on the beach, fishing and talking, and generally enjoying their lives.

Overall, Rockford and his father have a complicated but relatively functional relationship, and they take turns being the voice of reason when the other wants to do something ill-conceived. Their dynamic is the one reliable, endearing part of Rockford's life.

Beth Davenport

I don't want to make the claim that there are terrific female characters on *The Rockford Files* solely because there were women writing, directing, and producing the show. At the same time, I can't discount that the female characters on *The Rockford Files* are fully constituted in a way that was not happening on other 1970s television programs. Gretchen Corbett understood the depth and importance of Beth Davenport's character on the show: "There was something about the character Beth that I knew—it 'spoke' to me, because I'm a reasonably intelligent woman, and they didn't write such roles at the time."[9] Beth brings several important elements to *The Rockford Files*. Beth and Rockford have a deep personal relationship, having dated in the past, but during the present day of the show they are mostly friends and have an attorney-client relationship. Beth exists outside of her relationship with Rockford, but their interactions provide depth to their characters, Rockford's motivations, and his proclivities for finding legal trouble around every corner. In many episodes Beth works diligently to help Rockford and to give him advice about avoiding legal trouble in the first place. They express a deep affection for one another, as two friends who have seen the best and worst in each other. Their friendship also demonstrates great variability, in that they like each other as much as they annoy one another depending on the episode, much like Rockford's relationship with his father and his other friends. This dynamic crafts realism into the relationships on the program, that everyone's interactions with Rockford are nuanced, imperfect, and entertaining for viewers.

While Beth usually helps Rockford, Beth occasionally needs Rockford to help her, and these episodes help to explore her character and her relationships. This is demonstrated in the first episode in which Beth appears, the second episode of season one, "The Dark and Bloody Ground" (September 20, 1974). Here, Beth begs Rockford for his help and asks him to "donate" his detective services for one of her clients, Ann Calhoun (Patricia Smith), who has been accused of murdering her husband. Rockford's first interaction with Beth provides important character backstories. Beth attempts to persuade him by asking, "Don't you even care if she's innocent?" Rockford replies, "Beth, I spent five years in prison. While I was there, I never met anybody who wasn't innocent." Beth's line seems to appeal to Rockford's sense of right and wrong and indicate her hope that he might want to help prevent another innocent person from going to prison, harkening back to Rockford's underlying mission of helping those with less money and power find justice in the world. Rockford does agree to help, and he uncovers several layers of criminal acts in order to prove Calhoun's innocence. Again, like many of Rockford's clients, Beth ultimately can't pay him for his work clearing her client of murder charges but promises to pay him once Calhoun pays Beth. This episode also opens the door for Beth to return, as she asks Rockford at the end of the episode to work with her on another case, another penniless client, and though Rockford walks away in frustration, he nonetheless continues to work for Beth in many subsequent episodes.

Though Corbett appears as Beth in over thirty episodes, the season two episode "A Portrait of Elizabeth" (January 23, 1976) stands out as defining both Beth's character and her place in Rockford's life. In this episode Beth is dating Dave Delaroux (John Saxon), and she can't understand why Rockford doesn't like him. Later, while Rockford and

Beth attempts to lure Rockford away from fishing in "The Dark and Bloody Ground."

Beth are fighting after leaving an orchestra concert, Dave breaks into Rockford's trailer and kills two men in an elaborate scheme to implicate Rockford in fraud and murder. In this episode Beth shows many different sides, from her romantic relationship with Delaroux to her competence as an attorney: She tells the FBI agent Dan Shore (Wayne Tippit) "if you aren't absolutely straight about the way you handle this, I'm gonna hit you with half a dozen technicalities starting with failure to inform prisoner of his rights, and failure to grant consultation with counsel, and harassment." Once Rockford and several branches of law enforcement finally figure out that Dave is guilty of fraud and murder, Rockford and Beth are able to repair their friendship. During a long talk, Beth tells Rockford that she liked Dave, and Rockford seems to blame jealousy on why he treated Delaroux badly. She tells him that two years ago she thought Rockford was "the one," but then she says, "You're a tough catch. Sometime, I don't know, last year, I guess. I sort of settled for friend. And I started looking for someone with long-range possibilities. David looked like a good candidate." In this scene Beth reveals her feelings for Rockford, which demonstrates a vulnerability that she does not exhibit to other characters on the program and her difficulty moving on from their past romantic relationship.

In the episode "Crack Back" (March 25, 1977) Beth is representing Davey Woodhull (Howard McGillin), who has been charged with first-degree murder. Beth hires Rockford to track down Woodhull's date, who can alibi him for the night of the murder. Beth and Rockford have a complicated dynamic in this episode; she seems annoyed by his presence but needs his help on a case, causing him to be terse with Beth. Rockford is upset when Beth tells him that she hired another private investigator because "you were fishing. You're always fishing." Beth finally tells Rockford that her bad mood stems from feeling like she is being watched, and that someone is sending her secret gifts, all of which have rattled her ability to perform well as Woodhull's defense attorney. At first Beth is thrilled when Woodhull is found not guilty, but she quickly realizes that Rockford was correct in his theory

Rockford and Beth in "A Portrait of Elizabeth."

that Woodhull was responsible for the gifts and the stalking. Her anxiety turns to anger when she realizes that she just helped a murderer go free, but Woodhull is quickly arrested again for another murder. Interestingly, the end of this episode implies that Rockford and Beth restart their romantic relationship. Back at Rockford's trailer with Dennis and Rocky, Rockford tells Beth that he would like to call in his earlier rain check for dinner, and when she says she just wants to go back to her apartment, Rockford says, "Suits me" and they leave immediately. Again, the writing in this episode allows Beth's character to exhibit a range of emotions, showcasing Corbett's acting range and the multifaceted nature of this supporting character.

The season four episode "Forced Retirement" (December 9, 1977) features another storyline in which Beth feels violated and her expertise is questioned. The episode begins when she catches a man breaking into her apartment. This unknown intruder physically assaults her as he runs out the door. In the next shot Rockford is there comforting her, and he promises to help her investigate the assault. The main story in this episode revolves around her friend from Wellesley College, Susan Kenniston (Margie Impert), an engineer who has been working on a device to aid in underwater oil exploration. This episode provides Beth with additional backstory about her life before meeting Rockford. When Beth and Susan have lunch, their strained relationship shows through their somewhat contentious conversation, hinting at some checkered history from when they were classmates at Wellesley College. The mention of this alma mater, an exclusive private school, and their current professions, Beth is an attorney, and Susan an engineer, indicate their likely privileged upbringings. Working on this case has stirred up some long-simmering resentment between Susan and Beth, and it appears that these women are fighting over each other's success, though it is more complicated than this. At a meeting at Beth's law firm, Susan tells Beth that it seems as if she wants her to fail, and Beth's boss says, "Let's not have a catfight." Beth raises her voice, taking deep offense at the sexist accusation. Mark Alvey claims that Beth's character brought "a dash of seventies feminism to the show," demonstrated in this episode not only by her angry reaction at this sexist notion, but also later when she decides to quit her firm to go into private practice.[10] Beth mentions that she is worried about finding enough clients, and Rockford says, "They'll come, they'll come. And you know you've always got me." Beth replies, "Thanks Jim. I was talking about paying clients though," to which Rockford gives a very charming, surprised stare. Beth and Susan's underhanded rivalry arises again here when they quibble over Susan's ongoing legal case. Though perhaps not an entirely flattering moment in Beth's life, "Forced Retirement" does imbue more nuance and backstory into her character.

Though the writers succeeded in establishing Beth's character through her many appearances on the show, she had a premature goodbye. The character's final appearance is in the season four episode "The Attractive Nuisance" (January 6, 1978). Corbett left *The Rockford Files* due to a contract dispute between Cherokee Productions, Garner's production company, and Universal, where she was under contract.[11] Corbett did return as Beth in several of the made-for-television movies that aired in the 1990s, which I discuss in the conclusion.

Dennis Becker

Police officer Dennis Becker appears in nearly every episode of *The Rockford Files* and returns for all eight of the made-for-television reunion movies that aired in the 1990s. Outside of Dennis's relationship with Rockford, he is a detective with Homicide and Robbery, later promoted to lieutenant. He's married to Peggy (Pat Finley) and has one son, Scotty, whom he mentions a lot but who rarely appears on-screen. He occasionally tries to use his job to connect with his son, such as when he tries to impress Scotty by telling him that he was hanging out with Frank Falcone at the police station, who Rockford works with in "A Good Clean Bust with Sequel Rights."

Rockford's friendship with Dennis is complex. They are a bit unstable at times; sometimes the two men appear to be dear old friends, and at other times Dennis treats Rockford with anger and contempt. Dennis insinuates that Rockford only talks to him when he needs something. Rockford's relationship with Dennis is perhaps one of the places in which *The Rockford Files* does align with clichés about private detective dramas—the contentious relationship with the police, but also the character's need to have a police officer contact to investigate some leads.

As with the other supporting characters, a few episodes explore Dennis's backstory in a way that elevates the character and the actor. The episode that establishes Beth and Rockford's relationship, "The Dark and Bloody Ground," also sets up Rockford's connection to Dennis. Since the early premise of the show was that Rockford only worked on closed cases (the writers soon moved away from this idea) he goes to Dennis to discuss a case:

ROCKFORD: Becker, you're just gonna have to get this case back from the DA. I mean, it won't hold. . . . Anybody could have walked in on him.

DENNIS: You know, it just hits me what this is all about. It's that flaky attorney, the one who collects lost causes like they were rare coins.

ROCKFORD: Beth Davenport.

DENNIS: That's the one. She's trying to con you into working for nothing again, right? And you figure we reopen the case, you're off the hook, right?

ROCKFORD: That's what I had in mind. I can see it's not going to work.

DENNIS: Damn right.

This exchange serves multiple purposes. For one, it demonstrates that Rockford and Dennis have known each other long enough that he can ask Dennis for favors. As well, it implies that Rockford has worked with Beth previously, and that the police think she is a "flaky attorney," though this characterization never materializes in the subsequent episodes. Finally, during this exchange, both Rockford and Dennis are smiling and not taking it too seriously. Rockford even winks at Dennis as he leaves.

Dennis is not always a lighthearted, playful friend to Rockford. Sometimes there is a sinister component to their relationship, such as in the season one episode "The Countess" (September 27, 1974). Here Rockford calls Dennis and asks for some information but realizes that Dennis is keeping him on the phone while Lieutenant Diel finishes the warrant to arrest Rockford for murder. Rockford tells him, "Dennis, I thought we were friends" and hangs up on him. Later Dennis tells Rockford that he didn't think he was guilty of murder, but he had to arrest him for the sake of preserving his job on the police force.

At the end of the episode, Lieutenant Diel asks Dennis, "You like this jerk, don't you?"[12] Dennis replies, "No, I don't like him. I owe him a punch in his belly, and I can't collect if he's doing time." It is unclear from these exchanges whether or not they are truly friends, or if Dennis is forced to lie about his friendship with Rockford to stay in the good graces of his boss. At the end of "The Countess" Dennis flashes Rockford a peace sign as they depart in the hallway, suggesting that Dennis does in fact like Rockford, and they continue to meet up socially outside of the police station for the remainder of the series.

At other times, Dennis parlays the favors he does for Rockford into tangible returns. In the episode "Find Me If You Can" (November 1, 1974) Dennis helps Rockford identify some fingerprints, telling him "it's no big thing. No forms to fill out. Nothing like that." Nonetheless, Dennis asks him for tickets to the Lakers game, and tells Rockford that he will take Rocky to the game. Here, the fact that Dennis knows Rockford's dad well enough to go to a basketball game with him does seem to indicate that their friendship is real and goes beyond the bounds of Dennis's police favors.

Dennis helps Rockford far more often than the other way around, though the episodes in which Rockford is able to assist Dennis are fascinating forays into Dennis's character and personal life. Two standout episodes demonstrate the real depth of the friendship between Rockford and Dennis. In the season two episode "The Farnsworth Stratagem" (September 19, 1975), Rockford, Dennis, and Peggy Becker drive to the hotel they invested in to get a room for a weekend of golf. After some confusion at the hotel, the Beckers realize that they have put a lot of money into an investment scam. Dennis tells Rockford, "Jimbo, we need you, man," and the two men partner to create what Dennis calls a "slick con" counter scam. Rockford builds the counter scam by claiming the mineral rights on the hotel's land and needs dozens of other people to effectively pull this off, including Beth's legal help, Rocky as a driller, and other friends to play along. Rockford sells the mineral rights to the landowner, which gives him enough money to refund all the bad investments, including those of his nemesis's wife Mrs. Diel, though Dennis won't tell Lieutenant Diel that Rockford recovered their money. Dennis trusts Rockford enough to allow him to go even deeper into the scheme, but not enough to clear Rockford's name with his fellow officers.

In another well-regarded episode, "The Becker Connection" (February 11, 1977), writer Juanita Bartlett, whom I discuss in the next chapter, highlights the financial parallels between Rockford and the Beckers. Dennis's wife, Peggy, has set up a surprise party for Dennis, and when he arrives home after work, he is angry and ungrateful for the attention, and takes it out on everyone at the party. The crowd at the party demonstrates that Dennis has many friends who want to celebrate with him, and a wife who cares about him, but he is only concerned with how much money the whole affair has cost them. Dennis gets called back into work and is accused of stealing drugs while on temporary duty with the Narcotics division, and he is suspended pending an investigation. Rockford takes Dennis out for a beer, and as they talk, Dennis discusses his childhood and his parents allocating his father's paychecks every two weeks into envelopes marked rent, food, and clothes. The implication here is that Dennis grew up somewhat poor, and that he had hoped to have more money as an adult. Dennis says that he and Peggy don't have enough for their envelopes. Dennis hires Rockford to help "investigate an investigation." With everybody's help, Rockford and Dennis solve this case, and Dennis is able to return to work as a detective. Together, these two Dennis-centric episodes provide motivation behind his grumpy demeanor, and much like Rockford, his adult life has perhaps not unfolded in the ways that he had envisioned.

For a program built around a private detective who questions the investigative work done by the police and rarely trusts them, Dennis is given a lot of screen time and dedicated episodes to help develop his character and mold him into a somewhat likeable, somewhat sympathetic character whom Rockford usually trusts.

Dennis prepares to leave his birthday party in "The Becker Connection."

Evelyn "Angel" Martin

Despite the ups and downs in their relationships, Rockford often works with and trusts Rocky, Beth, and Dennis, though this is not true of other people in Rockford's inner circle. The "friendship" between Rockford and Angel defies logic, even more so than Rockford's relationship with Dennis. While Dennis does often help Rockford, Rockford's relationship with Angel is the opposite, in that he almost always needs Rockford to help him get out of trouble, frequently saying, "Jimmy, you gotta help me." As James Lardner notes, "Angel is the sternest test to which human loyalty can be put—a scalawag, a hustler, a huckster, a complete worm with no measurable redeeming features, who has at some point in the distant past managed inexplicably to stake a claim on Rockford's friendship."[13] What made this seemingly unlikeable character likeable is the actor who portrays him, Stuart Margolin, who won two Emmy Awards for playing Angel. As Richard Meyers notes, "Margolin made Angel the best-loved weasel of the decade—the man you love to hate and laugh at."[14] As with a few different actors on *The Rockford Files*, Margolin wasn't the first choice. As Garner notes in his memoir, "NBC didn't want Stuart in the show, but I was crazy about him and we cast him in the pilot as a snitch. NBC said they didn't like his performance, but we put him in a second episode anyway, then a third. NBC still didn't want him and they told us point-blank not to use him again. Then he got an Emmy nomination."[15]

From the limited backstory about their friendship, we know Angel and Rockford were in prison together in San Quentin, and thus Angel is one of Rockford's closest associates who understands what it was like to serve time in prison.[16] Throughout the series they interact with one another as old friends, though the pilot did feature a few telling lines of dialogue that would have been long ago discussed while the two men were still in prison. In the show's initial made-for-television movie "Backlash of the Hunter" (March 27, 1974) Angel tells Rockford, "I did that bank job," and asks him, "What about you, did you do that thing?" Rockford replies, "No, I was bad rapped." While this line is necessary to establish their relationship, it goes against the notion that they are old friends. It does, however, demonstrate Rockford's innocence and his private detective work parallel to an imperfect criminal justice system.

Occasionally Rockford needs Angel to find information about a person or a case, and he usually offers Angel small sums of money for his work, though Angel nearly always tries to hustle more money out of Rockford with his scheming. Angel does help Rockford when they are working to pull off their occasional "slick con" jobs, such as in "The Farnsworth Stratagem" and "Never Send a Boy King to Do a Man's Job" (March 3, 1979). Unlike Angel, Rockford's schemes are not in the service of enriching himself, as evidenced by his meager earnings and modest lifestyle. Rather, they are designed as countermeasures to help save friends and their families from other scammers.

Angel shows up frequently on *The Rockford Files*, usually causing mayhem here and there. Angel is not always the center of the action, but there are some episodes built entirely around his character and the troubles he causes for Rockford, such as in the episode "Chicken Little Is a Little Chicken" (November 14, 1975), which begins with Angel hiding money in Rockford's car door. After two guys kidnap Rockford and Angel and try to kill them, Rockford realizes that it was all an elaborate scheme to set up Angel. Rockford tries to walk away, saying, "I am through Angel. . . . Every time I look around, I stumble over one of your mistakes. . . . You deserve this frame. It was built for a dummy and it looks good on you." To get Rockford's help Angel promises he'll go straight after he figures out this mess. Rockford ends up with illegal counterfeit materials, and after getting arrested because of Angel, Rockford says, "I'm in here because I tried to help you, but you never leveled with me. . . . We ended up in so deep we're lucky we didn't get killed. And all because you didn't come clean with me. As far as I'm concerned Angel, we're through. That's it. You and I are quits." Of course, despite the intense amount of trouble that Angel causes Rockford, they remain friends, even into the 1990s reunion made-for-television movies.

In "Rattlers' Class of '63" (November 26, 1976) Angel continues his streak of manipulating everyone around him to make money illegally. The episode begins with Angel getting married to Regine (Elayne Heilveil), though in typical Angel fashion he doesn't want to pay more than ten dollars for his bride's ring. By the first night of their marriage, he tells Rockford that they are on the rocks, and later as Rockford tries to console Regine, he calls Angel "unique" twice, a fitting moniker for a character unlike any other on *The Rockford Files*. Naturally, the marriage is part of a much larger scam having to do with fake land sales for a brewery, part of which included Angel marrying Regine to secure the land. The drama created in this episode by Angel's money-making scheme is typical of the trouble he tends to cause Rockford, but there are several minutes at the end of the episode during which the viewer gets a glimpse of Angel's sincerity and honesty. In Rockford's trailer, Angel and Regine discuss their feelings for one another despite the annulment in progress. Angel begins to lie to her the way he lies to everyone, but he stops himself and admits he is lying. He tells her the truth about their marriage, that he did like her and wanted to be with her but was afraid of being killed. Angel suggests that they reconcile, but Regine says no and walks away. The closing image, of Regine and Rockford outside smiling, with Angel lingering in the background at the trailer's door, does allude to the fact that Rockford's drama and turmoil sometimes have a neutral ending—relief that he is not in jail because of Angel!

This ending freeze-frame image mirrors many closing shots of episodes of the show. Things are okay for both Rockford and Angel—they

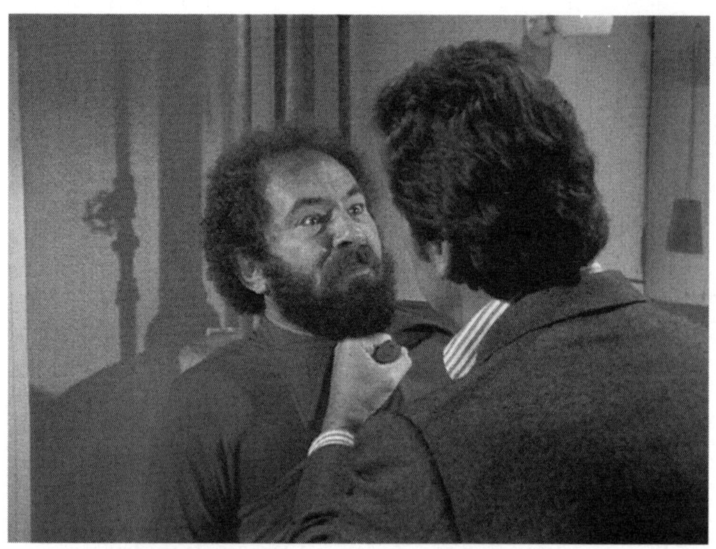

Angel creating trouble for Rockford in "Rattlers' Class of '63."

aren't currently in much trouble—but the "normal" life of marriage, romantic relationships, and stability eludes both men. Both men choose to continue in their careers, Rockford as a private investigator, Angel as a hapless, ineffective con man. Angel only truly succeeds at getting into trouble. He is fired by his brother-in-law, who owns a newspaper. He hilariously fails doing stand-up comedy at an open mic night in "The Becker Connection." He fails at marriage. He fails to be a loyal friend to anyone in his life, but even as this deeply flawed person, he was a popular character.

In all, these four supporting characters, all themselves fully fleshed out beyond just their relationships with Rockford, brought depth to Rockford's character and to the stories presented throughout the run of *The Rockford Files*.

2
"UNLIKE ANY PRIVATE EYE SERIES THAT HAD EVER BEEN DONE"

The Rockford Files's success with audiences came about through the collective inventiveness of Roy Huggins and Stephen J. Cannell that I discussed in the introduction, and the on-screen performers who brought the characters to life that I detailed in chapter one.[1] In addition to Huggins and Cannell, there was another group of individuals, from producers to writers, whose creative work shaped and defined *The Rockford Files*. The program employed executive producer and director Meta Rosenberg and writer Juanita Bartlett, two women with extensive creative control working at a time when female writers, producers, and directors were overlooked and underutilized.[2] According to Jennifer Keishin Armstrong, in 1973 only 6.5 percent of the people working behind the scenes on prime time television were women.[3] In her 1976 *Good Housekeeping* article, Muriel Davidson writes that James Garner was "a subliminal but dedicated women's libber."[4] Garner affirms his admiration of the women in his life, noting, "I love it that my life is propelled by my executive producer Meta Rosenberg, by my script genius Juanita Bartlett and by my wife and two daughters, Kim and Gigi."[5]

This chapter examines Cannell, Rosenberg, and Bartlett's roles on *The Rockford Files*, as well as two other people who contributed to the success of the show: David Chase and Charles Floyd Johnson. Chase, best known today for creating *The Sopranos* (1999–2007), began his career in the 1970s writing for television, and joined *The Rockford Files* in season three. Finally, Johnson served as a producer for one hundred episodes of the show's original run as well as executive producer for all eight of *The Rockford Files* CBS made-for-television movies in the 1990s. Johnson was also in charge of writing the infamous answering machine messages that appear at the beginning of each episode. Many of the elements that made this TV Milestone series distinctive came about because of the creative team behind *The Rockford Files*.

Stephen J. Cannell

Series co-creator Stephen J. Cannell began selling television scripts as a freelance writer in the late 1960s and later was hired as a story editor and writer on *Adam-12*. As Dennis Broe notes, Cannell "cut his Hollywood teeth writing *Adam-12*, where he learned the rules of the police docudrama only to subsequently and gleefully break them."[6] In the years leading up to *The Rockford Files* Cannell wrote for several other police-detective programs, including *Ironside*, *The D.A.* (1971–72), *Jigsaw* (1972–73), *Madigan* (1972–73), *Columbo* (1971–78), and *Toma*.

Stephen J. Cannell's signature style is in his ability to work within the conventions of the police and detective genre, while also incorporating new elements that challenge and shift these stories in novel ways. Cannell's writing centers on placing unique characters in entertaining situations but also acknowledging the serious undertones of these stories. His writing also balances comedic elements with dramatic storylines, extending genre experimentation to the level of character in addition to setting and iconography. Cannell demonstrated this creativity across many different episodes of *The Rockford Files*, but none more so than "White on White and Nearly Perfect" (October 20, 1978), which he wrote and directed. This episode is comically self-reflexive and harkens back to Cannell's comments about how his relationship with his father helped him form the father-son interactions between Rocky and Rockford. In this episode Rockford works closely with Lance White (Tom Selleck), who is the opposite of nearly every aspect of Rockford's work and existence. Lance is both clichéd and "nearly perfect," a replica of Joe Mannix, a character Cannell used as an antithesis for Rockford's character. The *Mannix* references are bountiful, such as when Lance tells Rockford that he is working for three eight-year-old boys, a nod to Cannell's anecdote about Mannix working for a little girl for "candy and quarters."[7] Lance also has an African American assistant, Maggie (Freddye Chapman), a connection to Mannix's assistant Peggy Fair, played by African American actress Gail Fisher. Unlike Rockford, Lance White is bound by his strict ethical code, which propels him to stand up to the villains in this episode and to interact pleasantly with Lieutenant Chapman, without receiving the bodily harm usually inflicted on Rockford during his investigations. By the end of the episode Lance marries into a wealthy family that gives him their lucrative business to run. For Rockford, he stumbles into his usual ending as well—his client decides not to give him a bonus payment. With the contrast between the two men, Cannell is able to use Rockford and Lance to explore how different people exercise their moral and ethical codes. The humor in this episode is rooted in the contrast between Rockford and Lance, but beneath this humor is a more serious statement. Rockford is reminded that he has to maneuver the world differently because of his ex-con past, especially as compared with Lance White's preposterous luck and optimism. Rockford exists in a world that sees only good intentions in the actions of men like Lance White, and only bad intentions in men like him.

Another episode, "Heartaches of a Fool" (September 22, 1978), highlights some themes that are present throughout Cannell's writing. In this episode, Cannell demonstrates the idea of authenticity and characters remaining true to their individual moral centers.

Here, Rocky and Rockford connect with country singer Charlie Strayhorn (Taylor Lacher) when Rocky has to fight with his trucking union to retain his insurance benefits after he is accused of causing an accident with his truck. Rocky has spent his career being a highly reliable, safe, union truck driver, and refuses to accept that he did something wrong. Charlie realizes that he doesn't like the life he is leading, of concert tours and serving as an object used by the people around him to make money. Rockford, of course, follows his instincts to seek justice by investigating what really happened with Rocky's accident, uncovering the dishonest marketing connected to a product being sold under Charlie's name, and helping both men repair and rebuild their reputations—much like the work that Rockford performs for his clients and himself in most episodes.

After *The Rockford Files* Cannell continued to write for many different types of law enforcement and private investigation television programs during his career, such as *Tenspeed and Brownshoe* (1980), as well as "amateur" detectives in the program *Hardcastle and McCormick* (1983–86).[8] In the 1990s he shifted away from writing television to writing mystery novels.[9] Cannell is remembered as "one of television's most prolific writers and series creators" with a lasting legacy in programs like *The Rockford Files*.[10]

Meta Rosenberg

By the time James Garner signed on to star on *The Rockford Files*, Meta Rosenberg had long served as Garner's agent, beginning after his work on *Maverick*.[11] According to Mollie Gregory, in the early 1970s "Rosenberg was one of the most powerful women working in television."[12] Rosenberg's work with Garner propelled her to serve as executive producer on *The Rockford Files*, and she also directed six episodes of the series. As Ed Robertson writes, Rosenberg had a "reputation as a tough-negotiating agent before becoming Garner's partner in Cherokee Productions."[13] Following her death in December 2004, Rosenberg's obituary in the *Los Angeles Times* included a quote from

David Chase to commemorate her: "She led an extraordinary adventure of a life through the force of her personality, her genius and her charm. She was a successful woman in a 'man's' industry."[14] Some accounts from people working in the entertainment industry acknowledge that Rosenberg was a woman working in a male-dominated industry, and thus the accusations of her being "tough" or "pushy" reflect the times more so than her professional demeanor. Rosenberg herself noted, "There were no women executives at that time, so I was kind of a freak . . . but because I was young enough and arrogant enough, I got along."[15]

What complicates Rosenberg's legacy with regard to her career success are events that transpired long before her work on television. Rosenberg began working in the 1940s as a story editor for 20th Century Fox and later "became head of the story department at Paramount."[16] Her obituary skips over a part of her life that has already been discussed at length—prior to the 1950s Rosenberg was a member of the Communist Party, and was issued a subpoena to testify to the House Un-American Activities Committee (HUAC) in 1951, where she complied with the committee and gave them names of current and former members of the Communist Party, some of whom were subsequently blacklisted from working in film, radio, and television. Her status as a "cooperative witness" who "named names" with HUAC and the fallout from this time in her life followed her, even after her death.[17] As Mollie Gregory notes in her study of pioneering women in the media industries, "Survivors from that era have strong feelings about Meta Rosenberg, both for and against."[18] However, the focus in this book is on her specific contributions to *The Rockford Files*, which began over twenty years after her controversial choice to testify.

Over the six seasons of the show's original run, Rosenberg directed six episodes, many of which I already discussed in the previous chapter. It can be difficult to look at six episodes of a show and talk about Rosenberg's directing style and what made her episodes unique. In many ways, these six episodes contain the same elements as nearly all

The Rockford Files episodes: Rockford investigates a case and finds trouble; there is a car chase between Rockford and someone connected to his investigation; Rocky, Beth, or Dennis gets angry at Rockford for some personal or professional reasons; followed by a resolution that wraps up the drama by the end of the episode. Within this story repetition, the creative team behind the show consistently found ways to include elements that challenged the conventions of the private detective genre.

One type of scene stands out from Rosenberg's adept direction: she creates emotionally raw exchanges in which two characters reveal personal information to one another for the first time, such as in her directorial debut, "A Portrait of Elizabeth" (January 23, 1976). As I noted in the previous chapter, this Beth-centric episode contains a scene during which Beth and Rockford have a lengthy conversation about their on-again, off-again romantic relationship. As the director of this episode, Rosenberg effectively filmed this scene to showcase its importance for character development, as Beth and Rockford rarely talk about anything personal between them. Rosenberg frames Beth at the center of the screen in a medium close-up long take. Rockford holds her tightly as she talks, and he listens patiently as she shares some heartbreaking details about her past relationship with Rockford and her desire to have a more typical romantic relationship. The quiet pensiveness of the characters in this scene amplifies new dimensions for both Beth and Rockford. It signifies the program's ability to blend comedy and drama but still retain a sincerity to its characters' feelings and actions and reveals a depth to these characters in a genre that often forgoes such exploration.

Rosenberg directed another character-building showcase in the season three episode "Rattlers' Class of '63" (November 26, 1976), when Angel and Regine discuss the annulment of their very short marriage. Drawing on the breadth of Stuart Margolin's acting abilities playing Angel, Rosenberg uses this slow, emotional scene for a rare moment when a character tells Angel that his constant scheming has negatively affected their life, and Angel actually listens and admits how easy it is for him to lie. This scene frames Angel and Regine together in a medium close-up shot, letting the viewer concentrate on the characters and their performances through not just dialogue, but facial expressions. Here, Angel almost appears to change, if briefly, into a person who feels remorse for hurting someone in his life. Angel looks hurt and diminished at the end of the conversation, perhaps ready to change, but it is fleeting, because he returns to his old self in the next episode in which his character appears. Rosenberg again uses these intense interactions to emphasize emotional depth that exists beneath the surface of these characters.

Playing on her directorial strengths with this type of scene, Rosenberg again stages a slow-moving scene that allows Rockford to listen and show compassion for a friend. In "There's One in Every Port"

Angel and Regine discuss their relationship in "Rattlers' Class of '63."

(January 7, 1977), Rockford goes to visit his friend Eddie (Howard Duff) in the hospital, and their conversation references the time they spent together in prison, while also addressing Eddie's failing health. The scene feels much like the emotional exchange in the previous Rosenberg-directed episodes, another moment of character development between friends. However, Rockford realizes that Eddie was faking his illness when he returns to the hospital to find a note reading, "After all, you should have seen this one coming. Love, Eddie." This twist doesn't negate Rockford's genuine feelings and sympathy he expressed for his friend Eddie but does remind viewers that even Rockford occasionally lets his emotions override his naturally skeptical demeanor.

Rosenberg directed three additional episodes, including two written by David Chase: "Quickie Nirvana" (November 11, 1977) and "The Queen of Peru" (December 16, 1977). The sixth and final episode Rosenberg directed was "Local Man Eaten by Newspaper" (December 8, 1978), which was written by Juanita Bartlett. In the next section I will discuss Bartlett, who had thirty-three writing credits on *The Rockford Files* over its six original seasons and wrote several of the 1990s made-for-television movies that aired on CBS.

Juanita Bartlett

When Juanita Bartlett became a writer and producer for television, there were few women working in these capacities. According to Meta Rosenberg in her interview with the Television Academy in 1998, Juanita Bartlett began working with Rosenberg as her secretary, and during that time, Bartlett wrote a script for *Nichols* that Rosenberg thought was "really very good."[19] Bartlett would go on to write several more episodes for *Nichols*, as well as scripts for *Toma* and *Little House on the Prairie* (1974–83). At *The Rockford Files* Bartlett served as a writer, story editor, producer, and supervising producer. Co-creator Roy Huggins noted that he "liked working with Bartlett" because he felt that she could "take an original story of his and 'actually make it better.'"[20] According to Ed Robertson, "Huggins was a pioneer . . . at Universal: At a time when television writing was still very much a male-driven profession, he often hired female writers for his shows."[21] Bartlett and Huggins seem to have had a mutually respectful relationship. Bartlett told Robertson in a separate interview that Huggins "was a nice man and very talented. He used me a lot. It didn't scare him that I was a woman. Prejudice against female writers existed at the time but it didn't exist for Roy. He gave me a chance when other people wouldn't. It changed my life."[22]

Bartlett's scripts for *The Rockford Files* are well regarded. James Garner noted in his memoir that Bartlett "wrote some of the best" episodes of the show, including "The Great Blue Lake Land and Development Company" (October 17, 1975), which focused on land fraud, and "So Help Me God" (November 19, 1976), an episode that exposed issues with grand juries.[23] The Writers Guild nominated "So Help Me God" for Best Episodic Drama in 1976. These types of episodes, in which Rockford's investigations explore contemporary social issues, will be discussed in chapter three.

There are several narrative threads that flow through Bartlett's scripts across the series. First, her scripts often center on social issues by focusing on the "underdogs," the overlooked, the people whose experiences mirror Rockford's own struggles with injustice. These episodes also show Rockford bending or breaking the law, though always in the service of helping people, in an unspoken "ends justify the means" manner. Even in these moments in which Rockford skirts the law, the characters are humanized and written in such a way that the audience roots for Rockford and his clients. Again, this is a strength of having the character work as a private investigator, rather than a police officer, the latter of which would be unable to break the law on-screen without serious ramifications.

Many of Bartlett's scripts share a narrative angle that makes her episodes stand out. While the very essence of the series depicts Rockford working alone as a private detective, several of the episodes penned by Bartlett pair Rockford with a female lead who both helps and hinders his investigations. These "helpers" mirror Cannell's work to alter the typical conventions of the private detective as a loner. Cannell gave Rockford an involved father, and Bartlett continued this trajectory by providing Rockford with investigative assistants. Rather than writing these "helpers" as Rockford's romantic partners, they are almost always partners in crime, either overtly "pulling a job" with Rockford or in underhanded ways attempting to trick him, such as withholding information or assuming a false identity.

One female "helper" episode involves an elaborate, partially illegal scheme to extricate the Beckers from financial troubles. In the season two episode "The Farnsworth Stratagem" (September 19, 1975), which I discussed in the previous chapter in terms of Dennis's character development, the Beckers ask Rockford to help them recover their money from what proves to be a real-estate investment scam. Rockford is approached by Audrey Wyatt (Linda Evans), who says she has lost money in the scam as well. Audrey and Rockford construct an elaborate ruse to find oil, gas, and minerals on the property and then sell the mineral rights back to the people who orchestrated the real-estate scam. Over the course of their scheme, Rockford realizes that Audrey did not lose money on the scam but was part of the original swindle. They continue to work together, but Rockford grows more guarded in their partnership. Rockford goes back to his usual existence as a private detective after their temporary partnership, and Audrey thanks him for not turning her in to the police. The undercurrent in "The Farnsworth Stratagem" is that Audrey seems to have some remorse after the whole ordeal but tells Rockford that the experience "changed her perspective, but it won't change my life." After this episode, Rockford also continues transgressing the boundaries of the law, refusing to shift his career into anything his father might find more respectable.

While Bartlett wrote several female co-investigator episodes, their stories all unfold in unique ways. Depending on the episode,

Rockford either immediately trusts or is suspicious of the clients who come to him for help. In "The Farnsworth Stratagem" he begins by trusting Audrey and only grows to distrust her after catching her in several lies. In "Resurrection in Black & White" (November 7, 1975), co-written with Stephen J. Cannell, Susan Alexander (Joan Van Ark) hires Rockford to help exonerate Dave Kruger (John Lawlor), who is in prison after being convicted of murdering his girlfriend, Cheryl Wilson. Rockford doesn't so much distrust Susan as he believes she is wasting her time on a guilty man. Rockford agrees to work with Susan, and they begin to explore a complicated case, with missing police files, an attorney with memory loss after a stroke, and a faked murder for insurance money. While the characters on *The Rockford Files* do not often speak about Rockford's time in prison or his pardon from the governor, episodes such as "Resurrection in Black & White" allow Rockford to help other innocent people who have been wrongfully convicted. This is the core motivation of his investigative work, even though Rockford subtly embodies this philosophy more than he articulates it to his friends, family, or clients.

In "The Girl in the Bay City Boys Club" (December 19, 1975) Rockford is asked to investigate a case that grows more complicated with each new clue he uncovers. This episode is the only one that James Garner directed in all his years on *The Rockford Files*. In his memoir Garner wrote that he "never wanted to direct" and that he preferred to "concentrate on acting."[24] Despite this fact, Garner incorporated some intriguing stylistic choices and camera movement into his one experience directing the show. The episode begins with Rockford at a poker game, posing as Mr. Keil, who is really Angel's brother-in-law. When he leaves the game, he is followed by a woman who later identifies herself as Kate Flanders (Blair Brown). The episode does not begin with Rockford teaming up with a female client to investigate a case. Instead, he meets with Mr. Phelps (Stewart Moss), who has hired Rockford to check out a rigged poker game at the Boys Club. The case here is multilayered, with many misdirection elements that keep circling back to the district attorney's office. Mr. Phelps is actually Burt Kimball, the deputy district attorney, and Kate Flanders is really Kate Doyle, who also works for the district attorney's office. While Kimball instigated the investigation, it switches to Rockford and Kate investigating Kimball. They pool their expertise in innovative ways—Kate shares information from the district attorney's office, and Rockford takes on a covert identity to find information by examining the Club's electrical bills. Instead of bending the law, Rockford fully breaks the law here by breaking into the Boys Club to look for a hidden camera being used to fix the poker games. The episode ends with an exchange about law breaking, between Rockford and Kate. Kate tells him, "You have a tendency to bend a lot of rules . . . carrying a lock pick, breaking, and entering. Destruction of private property. Those are all chargeable offenses." Rockford tells Kate, "Yeah, you

Rockford and Kate in "The Girl in the Bay City Boys Club."

know what's worse? I had an accomplice." Rockford's co-investigator Kate becomes his co-conspirator, a partner in crime, much like Susan Alexander in "Resurrection in Black & White."

Bartlett doesn't always write Rockford a "helper," but her episodes always feature cases that have multiple, complex layers of misdirection for him to uncover. For example, in the episode "Piece Work" (December 17, 1976), Rockford works alone in what at first is an insurance investigation that shifts into one looking into illegal guns. In "A Deadly Maze" (December 23, 1977) Rockford is hired to find a missing woman in what turns out to be a social-scientific experiment but nonetheless leads him to investigate a murder connected to the original case. In "The Fourth Man" (September 24, 1976) Lori Jenivan (Sharon Gless) teams up with Rockford after an incident at work that makes her suspect she is in danger. Lori had unintentionally stumbled on a contract killer, Timson Farrell (John McMartin), working to "eliminate" people who were about to testify to a senate committee, as part of an organized crime ring. In classic *The Rockford Files* style, Rocky talks Lori out of paying Rockford at the end of the episode.

Bartlett was also given the opportunity to write several episodes that feature a recurring guest star. Bartlett penned three episodes with a connected storyline around Rita Capkovic, played by "special guest star" Rita Moreno. For her portrayal of Capkovic, Moreno won the 1978 Emmy for Outstanding Lead Actress for a Single Appearance in a Drama or Comedy Series. In her speech Moreno spoke about Juanita Bartlett, saying that Bartlett was "a lady who really knows how to write about ladies."[25] In these episodes, Capkovic is a sex worker who has a lot in common with Rockford. They are loners in "unrespectable" professions, they find themselves in dangerous situations, and neither makes enough money to be financially secure, yet both are content enough with their lives. While Rockford never stops being a private detective, Capkovic finally wants to change her life and career after finding herself in mortal danger multiple times: she is beaten up, shot at, charged with murder, and stalked.

Capkovic first appears in "The Paper Palace" (January 20, 1978), when Dennis Becker bails her out of jail on an alleged prostitution charge. Capkovic tells Dennis that she is upset because he only sees her as an informant, but she sees him as a friend. He ends up inviting her over for a small dinner party, and it is awkward for everyone except Capkovic. Rockford drives Capkovic home and gets pulled into some trouble in her life. The men harassing her end up murdering her friend Maggie Gillson (Shirley O'Hara) because they have been embezzling money from her. Rockford uncovers what is going on and helps Capkovic out of danger, at least temporarily. She inherits $300,000 from Maggie, enough for her to find a new, safer way to support herself.

Capkovic appears again in "Rosendahl and Gilda Stern Are Dead" (September 29, 1978). She is charged with a murder she did not commit, and her friends help to bail her out. The investigation in this episode revolves around a medical malpractice accusation by Phil Gabriel (Abe Vigoda) against Rosendahl (William Joyce). There are some noteworthy connections in this episode to earlier Bartlett scripts. Much like Blair Brown's character Kate Doyle in "The Girl in the Bay City Boys Club" when she tells Rockford that all of the laws he is breaking are "chargeable offenses," Capkovic tells Rockford, "Do you know what the cops would do if they find that lock pick on you? It's illegal!" Rockford tells her, "Rita, on my best day, I'm borderline." The use of "borderline" is a Bartlett writing flourish, as she also uses it in "The Farnsworth Stratagem" when Audrey Wyatt says to Rockford, "The pearl switch, recording the combination to a safe . . . isn't that kind of illegal?" Rockford replies, "Oh, it's borderline."

Rita Moreno's character, Capkovic, makes her last appearance in the original series in the season six episode "No Fault Affair" (November 30, 1979), which was also Bartlett's last script for the original run of the series. Rita has gone to cosmetology school and is applying for jobs at salons. One of Rita's old acquaintances Al Haluska (Jerry Douglas) shows up, and when she says she is no longer in the sex worker business, he beats her up and leaves her on the side of the road. Haluska ends up shooting Rita, which provides Angel with a rare opportunity to have a heroic moment when he charges at Al after the shooting (before quickly running away from Al in classic Angel style). The scene cuts to a shot of a seagull flying in slow motion, before the shot dissolves into one with Dennis, Peggy, Rocky, and Angel fishing off the pier. This episode ends with some purposefully vague dialogue that keeps taking the short final scene in different directions. For a minute it seems that Rita is dead, and that the characters are having a moment of mourning, as Peggy says to the group, "How long are we supposed to do this? I mean, is that it? Don't we do anything?" It turns out that Peggy is not asking about when they stop memorializing Rita, but instead how long they will be there fishing. The characters then talk briefly about what happened when Rita was shot, and Peggy again asks, "Well, what happens now?" Rocky mentions that Rita will be going to work with a friend of his once she recovers from this new set of injuries. Peggy listens, but asks, "I meant, what happens with them?" and the shot cuts to Rita and Rockford holding hands on the beach, just talking about her next steps, wrapping up Rita's three-episode character arc. In all three Capkovic episodes Rockford focuses on fixing yet another injustice in the system, while bending the law in the process.

The themes present in Bartlett's scripts continue in the CBS made-for-television movies that aired in the 1990s, which I discuss in the conclusion. Bartlett's ability to step into a narrative universe created by Huggins and Cannell demonstrates her skills as a writer, yet she found her own novel ways to challenge the conventions of the private detective genre.

David Chase

David Chase became a regular writer on *The Rockford Files* in season three. Chase began his career in the 1970s writing for a television program that continues to have a dedicated fan base, *Kolchak: The*

Night Stalker (1974–75), the focus of another TV Milestones book.[26] Overall, Chase wrote seventeen episodes and produced sixty-five episodes of the original *The Rockford Files* series, with two additional credits for teleplay writing. In 2005 the Edgar Allan Poe Awards gave Chase a Special Edgars Award for his work on *The Rockford Files*. Much like Juanita Bartlett's writing career, which began with Meta Rosenberg reading one of her scripts, Rosenberg hired Chase as a writer and producer after reading one of his scripts that she deemed "terrific."[27] Victoria E. Johnson writes that after Chase joined *The Rockford Files* in season three, the show "began to be hailed as more 'literate' and smart, featuring more well-rounded characters, deeper (and darker) explorations of its hero's personal life—including story-lines that tackled broader social questions than previously had been considered."[28] While Chase wrote some popular and clever episodes of the series, I don't detect this tonal shift in season three. Rather, I think part of what makes *The Rockford Files* a TV Milestone is that it was consistently effective in its genre hybridity, its playfulness with the private detective conventions, and its ability to balance drama and comedy, dating back to its debut made-for-television movie.

Much like the story connections between Bartlett's scripts discussed in the previous section, Chase's episodes also have similar elements that he relied on repeatedly—all the way through his writing career up to and including *The Sopranos*—crime families, mental illness, characters adrift in their search for meaning in their lives, and psychotherapy, such as in the season four episode "The Dog and Pony Show" (October 21, 1977). On the surface this is a typical episode of *The Rockford Files* that begins with Rockford and Angel in a courtroom in front of a judge for theft charges. The judge sentences both men to jail but suspends the sentences if they seek psychiatric help. Angel and Rockford attend group therapy, after which one of the participants, Mary Jo (Joanne Nail), asks Rockford to investigate whether someone has been following her. Rockford investigates and it eventually leads him to a crime family desperately trying to hide a family member,

Joey B., who is struggling with mental illness. As Rockford attempts to extricate himself from this situation, Tommy Lorentz (George Loros) very melodramatically asks Rockford "why us? I mean, why is this family visited with mental illness?" hinting at some of the themes that David Chase would continue to explore throughout his career. Eventually, all is resolved, the bad guys are arrested, and Rockford and Mary Jo reconnect at their therapy session.

Three of the episodes Meta Rosenberg directed for *The Rockford Files* were written by David Chase.[29] In season four Rosenberg directed "Quickie Nirvana," a fascinating episode that allowed the main characters and guest stars to investigate a case unlike any other on the show. Like the Bartlett episodes that provide Rockford with a female investigative helper, the lead character in this episode, Sky Aquarian/Jane Patten/Gopi/Hester (Valerie Curtin) is, in theory, a helper, but mostly hinders Rockford, causing him trouble at every step in the investigation. She is a woman in search of a belief system, floating between different spiritual practices and jobs. In a typical episode Rockford relies on his ability to take on different personas in order to uncover information in his cases. Sky takes on a similar number of personas, but she appears to be in search of finding herself, which is tonally different from Rockford in a disconcerting way. By the end of the episode, Rockford finds her preaching about Jesus on a sidewalk, where she is attempting to sell books written by Reverend Goodhew. While the end of this episode is delightfully vague in some ways, it ends with the audience knowing that this will not be her final religious change, and that she will likely continue seeking multiple spiritual paths.

As I noted earlier, heart-to-heart conversations are a common element in Rosenberg's direction. Sky and Rockford have several short heart-to-heart conversations, such as one in which Sky points out the contradictions inherent in Rockford's life. He is mad about the neighborhood dogs messing with his garbage cans and complains about people not observing leash laws—quite a contradictory statement coming from a character who bends the law frequently. Sky says to him, "Leash laws? You're an unusual blend, Jim. You know, you're sweet, hang loose, and yet kind of a fascist." Earlier Sky had called him "kind of an enlightened guy," but she is upset at him for cleaning and cutting up a fish he caught. While the usual Chase element of the therapist is missing here, the many spiritual leaders who pop in and out of Sky's life in her existential search for meaning and her focus on using these beliefs to improve herself certainly fit within Chase's usual thematic fixations.

Chase returns to his enthrallment with therapy and therapists in "Black Mirror" (November 24, 1978). In this episode Rockford stumbles across a woman on the beach, Dr. Megan Dougherty (Kathryn Harrold), whom he asks out on a date, but she declines. Dougherty is a psychologist who also happens to be blind. She seeks Rockford out after someone physically assaults her outside of her office. Rockford seems quite enamored with Megan, as is Rocky, so much so that he compliments Rockford's career in front of her, in an attempt to impress her. Rocky says, "I was just saying what a good living he makes at being a detective, you know," which a regular viewer would recognize as something Rocky has *never* thought or said before. Chase wrote another episode that features Megan Dougherty, "Love Is the Word" (November 9, 1979), his penultimate script for *The Rockford Files*. In this episode Rockford and Dougherty's romantic relationship changes, but Rockford doesn't seem to recognize this until it is too late. Rockford is at Megan's house and is complaining about his life, and Megan manages to interrupt long enough to tell him that she is engaged to another man, Jeffrey Smith (Anthony Herrera). He later attends their wedding, and they make peace with their relationship having turned out much the same as his relationship with Beth—he is too busy and too focused on himself to be the traditional romantic partner that both women are seeking. In this regard Rockford does fall into the typical genre parameters of the loner private detective—though he has his dad, he seems destined to fail in terms of his romantic relationships.

David Chase wrote one of the last episodes of the program, "Just a Coupla Guys" (December 14, 1979), which was intended to be a spin-off but was not picked up by NBC. Rockford is in New Jersey on a case but rejects it once he discovers his client's connection to organized crime. The episode's parallel story is about Mickey Long (Gene Davis) and Eugene Conigliaro (Greg Antonacci), who are trying to insert themselves into an organized crime family. These "would-be hustlers" have a lot of ambition but aren't succeeding at their ultimate goal. This spin-off's focus is on these new characters, and not on Rockford, which makes it feel unbalanced. The episode was not well received by *Variety* critic Mick (Larry Michie), who noted that it had "the familiar 'Rockford' charm when Garner was on screen," but that he found it "lapsing into amateurish tedium when spinoff possibilities were being mined."[30]

This episode and several others of *The Rockford Files* written by Chase, in retrospect, feel like first drafts of what would later become *The Sopranos*, containing many of Chase's thematic elements that would populate his most popular television writing twenty years later. After *The Rockford Files* ended, and before Chase's success on HBO, he wrote for several other television programs, including *Northern Exposure* (1990–95) and *I'll Fly Away* (1991–93). He also penned two of *The Rockford Files* 1990s reunion made-for-television movies, including the aptly titled "Godfather Knows Best" (February 18, 1996), which I discuss in detail in the conclusion.

Charles Floyd Johnson

Charles Floyd Johnson served many roles on *The Rockford Files*, including over fifty producer credits, dozens of associate producer and supervising producer credits, and four "story by" credits. Johnson ended up working for the show through an odd series of events. He was an attorney working in Washington, DC, but wanted to work as an actor. After moving to Los Angeles, Johnson began working for Universal in the mail room, but only for three days. Michael E.

Hill notes that "equal employment opportunity pressures were on, and it wasn't long before Charles Johnson—black, with a law degree" was hired away to serve as a production coordinator at Universal.[31] In 2023 Johnson did an interview with the Television Academy in which he talks about being assigned to *The Rockford Files* and his great working relationship with Huggins, Garner, Cannell, Rosenberg, and Bartlett. When Huggins left the show, Rosenberg and Cannell asked Johnson to move into an associate producer role. Johnson noted in this interview "there were almost no associate producers of color on the lot. Later on, a couple of others joined me. But it was a trailblazing position, and I learned on the job."[32]

In his memoir James Garner writes that Johnson was "in charge of the notorious phone messages" that begin each episode of *The Rockford Files*.[33] Though these were popular with the audience and created as a stand-in to replace the traditional private detective secretary role, they were apparently difficult to write. Juanita Bartlett noted that "toward the end of our run, we were getting 'messaged out.' . . . Sometimes it was a matter of 'if you have any ideas, come see us, please.'"[34] While the producers and writers had difficulty coming up with ideas by the end of the show, Johnson notes that "we all had fun writing them."[35] These messages were, and are still, treasured by fans of the program, yet they also function as brief moments of character development for Rockford and glimpses into his complicated life. This is demonstrated in the episode "The Countess" (September 27, 1974): The message is "hey, Rockford, very funny. I ain't laughin'. You're gonna get yours," vaguely implying that Rockford has done something wrong and that someone wants to exact their revenge on him. In "Coulter City Wildcat" (November 12, 1976) the answering machine message tells the story of a man too busy to remember to keep his plants alive: "It's Shirley at the Plant and Pot. There's no easy way to tell you this Jim. We did everything we could. . . . Your fern died."

Johnson's four "story by" credits sum up the collaborative nature of the creative contributors for *The Rockford Files*. Juanita Bartlett wrote the teleplays for two of Johnson's story credits, "Deep Blue Sleep" (October 10, 1975) and "The Becker Connection" (February 11, 1977) (story by Johnson and Ted Harris). Stephen J. Cannell wrote the teleplay for "Foul on the First Play" (March 12, 1976) (story by Johnson with Dorothy J. Bailey), and Cannell and David Chase co-wrote the teleplay for "The Prisoner of Rosemont Hall" (February 17, 1978) (story by Johnson and Maryann Rea). Since his time with *The Rockford Files* Johnson has continued to work as a producer on a number of prominent television programs, including *Magnum, P.I.* (1980–88), *Quantum Leap* (1989–93), *JAG* (1995–2005), *NCIS* (2003–), and the 1990s *Rockford* made-for-television movies that aired on CBS.

Together, these central creative figures behind many of the show's most beloved scripts demonstrate the collaborative space that *The Rockford Files* afforded women writers and people of color at a time before executives prioritized highlighting diverse voices. They also represent a team that worked together to craft characters, episodes, and scenes that made the most of the playful genre hybridity that defined *The Rockford Files*. While none of the five people discussed in this chapter appear on-screen on *The Rockford Files*, they remain integral parts of the overall success of the program.

3
"THE STORIES HAVE SUBSTANCE"

A 1978 advertisement in *The Hollywood Reporter* noted that one strength of *The Rockford Files* was that "the stories have substance" and this was one of several reasons the show was worthy of "Emmy consideration."[1] As James Lardner describes it, *The Rockford Files* "has a way of creeping up on substantial questions."[2] Another critic, Howard Rosenberg, wrote an article praising the show as "the era's best detective series," but opined that when *The Rockford Files* "occasionally tackled social issues" it had "fallen on Garner's face."[3] Somewhere between James Lardner and Howard Rosenberg's differing assessments of the television program, many of the show's most celebrated episodes successfully tackled issues involving the criminal justice system, grand juries, organized crime, feminism, gun rights, violence on television, real-estate fraud, and the increasingly intrusive uses of technology for surveillance purposes. In this chapter I focus on how *The Rockford Files* delved into contemporary social issues, and how many of these problems continue to resonate half a century later. Writers Stephen J. Cannell and Juanita Bartlett adeptly integrated these social issues into Rockford's everyday life and work, while also framing the investigation to suggest that these issues go far beyond the scope of just one person.

The causes that define Rockford's worldview unfold through his investigative work from the very beginning of the show. In the made-for-television movie that served as the show's pilot, "Backlash of the Hunter" (March 27, 1974), Sara Butler (Lindsay Wagner) asks Rockford to investigate her father's death after the police have written it off as a "dead ender" case, because Butler's dad was homeless with substance use issues. This episode begins with the murder happening on-screen, much like a typical episode of *Columbo*, so the audience already knows there is more to Sara's father's death than the police have concluded, and Rockford's intervention here is warranted. From the first instances of Rockford's character appearing on-screen, his work to fight the injustices of the world is put into action and shown to be necessary in an environment where the police deem certain cases not important enough to investigate fully. Rockford puts effort into these investigations even when the police do not—though it rarely leads to a paycheck. While Sara Butler's case involved the death of her father, the focus on the lack of police attention to cases like his speaks to the program's stance on inequality and injustice in its narrative universe. These types of episodes demonstrate that the program not only experimented with genre hybridity, but that it also set itself apart from its contemporaries by having Rockford investigate challenging cases that highlighted real-world issues.

In James Garner's memoir, he notes that Juanita Bartlett wrote two standout episodes of the show, "The Great Blue Lake Land and Development Company" (October 17, 1975) and "So Help Me God" (November 19, 1976), based on stories she had watched on *60 Minutes*.[4] The episode "The Great Blue Lake Land and Development Company" begins with Rockford stumbling into some bad luck, which leads to him uncovering real-estate fraud and murder. Rockford's car breaks down and he is forced to stay in a rural motel for the night. Concerned about the amount of cash he is carrying for a client, Rockford puts the money in the town's only safe, at a company selling real-estate plots in the desert. When the money is not in the safe the next day, the sheriff and the company's owner accuse Rockford of falsifying the record of his deposit. Suspecting there is something underhanded going on, Rockford asks Rocky to go undercover to the company to ask for a tour and to listen to a presentation about the land they are selling. Rocky is upset after investigating and tells Rockford, "They're selling an invisible lake," deeply troubled by the idea of the company making off with the life savings of retirees. By the end of the episode, Rockford has uncovered several layers of fraud with the land company and managed to get the sheriff to drop the unfounded murder charges against him. The episode features two important issues, fraud in terms of selling useless land, and people taking financial advantage of retirees. It concludes on a satisfying note in that Rockford is set free, and the unscrupulous land sellers will be held accountable for breaking the law.[5] Rockford does not always achieve this level of justice in his cases, but the writers occasionally allow his character a level of professional accomplishment.

Juanita Bartlett's other *60 Minutes*–inspired episode, "So Help Me God," conveys to the audience a call for action in its scathing commentary on grand jury proceedings. In this episode Rockford receives a subpoena to appear before a federal grand jury. After consulting with his attorney Beth, he begins answering the grand jury's questions about Frank Sorvino, a man Rockford claims not to know. One of the attorneys, Gary Bevins (William Daniels), berates Rockford with questions, and then in an attempt to embarrass or attack Rockford, asks him to talk about why he had been in prison. Rockford refuses to disclose anything and instead uses the Fifth Amendment but is charged with civil contempt for not answering. Beth tells him he has to cooperate or risk being in jail for at least nine months until the grand jury term expires. He tells Beth, "I haven't been charged with anything; I haven't been convicted of anything. . . . Do you realize how long I could be in here?" Beth is able to get Rockford out temporarily based on a mistake on the original subpoena, so Rockford uses his time and freedom to investigate what is really happening with the case. When he is subpoenaed a second time, he is again charged with contempt and ends up in prison. The underlying case here is that Sorvino faked his kidnapping to escape the consequences of embezzling money from his union. Before Rockford has a chance to inform the prosecutor about his findings, he is attacked in prison and stabbed, ending up at the hospital. Once he recovers, Rockford appears before the grand jury for a third time and is quickly dismissed. The presiding juror agrees to let Rockford make a statement. Rockford delivers a short speech about a case that he says he read about recently. He quotes the article: "There is no such thing as a small injustice. There is no such thing as a minor abridgement of rights. That if even one citizen is so deprived, make no mistake, we all suffer." The attorney who charged him multiple times with contempt, Bevins, is annoyed that Rockford now won't leave the witness stand, but Rockford ends his statement by telling him that he was quoting Bevins. The episode ends with an intertitle that reads, "The abuse of the Federal Grand Jury system as dramatized here is currently permissible under existing laws," a strong statement directed at the audience at the end of this somber episode.

Though Garner is often credited as being a talented actor who is adept at blending comedy and drama in his performances, the seriousness of this episode—with a stabbing that nearly kills him, and his rights being subverted by the grand jury—showcases both Garner's acting abilities and Bartlett's writing. The episode is at once satisfying and frustrating—Rockford perseveres, but in order to do so he ends up back in prison, a terrible sacrifice for someone who has already served five years in prison for a crime he did not commit. This episode, and others that examine the criminal justice system, are deeply concerned with the inner workings of the law; how unevenly it is wielded by the police, the courts, and attorneys; and how powerless people can feel when trapped in legal intricacies that an average person may not understand. The issues examined in this episode, and many other episodes of *The Rockford Files*, always come back to issues of class–it takes money to afford effective attorneys who can help a client navigate an unfair system. Rockford can't really afford to pay Beth, but she works with him out of an ongoing friendship. Rockford is punished for trying to push back against yet another injustice. Yet Bevins is not punished for falsely accusing Rockford of being a part of the conspiracy at the heart of these grand jury proceedings.

Within the context of this fictional television show, episodes like "So Help Me God" convey that the writers saw the show as a vehicle for change by educating viewers about contemporary issues. In a 1977 article written for *The New York Times*, "Bar Group Urges Help for Grand Jury Witnesses," Warren Weaver Jr. notes that the American Bar Association was imploring Congress to "adopt a broad program of grand jury changes aimed at abuses by prosecutors and providing more protection for witnesses."[6] While not necessarily in reference to the *60 Minutes* story that inspired "So Help Me God," Weaver's article demonstrates that issues with grand jury proceedings were under discussion in the 1970s.

The threat and lingering trauma of prison inform Rockford's character at a deep, unspoken level. Much like Rockford's uneven reintegration back into society after his pardon from the governor, other characters struggle to resume their lives after prison. Rockford is different from many of the ex-cons that populate his universe. His post-prison life choices, though not entirely legal, are largely rooted in maintaining his private detective business. Other characters, such as Angel, continue to try to make money illegally (even though he is not terribly effective at being a con artist). Rockford's friend Eddie, from "There's One in Every Port" (January 7, 1977), also continues his life of crime after his time in prison. Similarly, in "The Farnsworth Stratagem" (September 19, 1975) Audrey chooses to continue her illegal activities even after befriending some of the victims of her financial scam.

The pursuit of life after prison, and each character's personal choices about their futures, are at the center of the episode "The

Hammer of C Block" (January 9, 1976). Here, Rockford comes home to his trailer and finds Gandolph "Gandy" Fitch (Isaac Hayes), a man who had served time with Rockford. Gandy is having trouble reintegrating into society after having served twenty years in prison for the murder of his girlfriend Lilah McGee, a crime he insists he did not commit. Since Rockford owes Gandy $1,500, which he doesn't have, Gandy hires Rockford as a trade to figure out who really killed Lilah. Rockford uncovers that Gandy and Lilah had an abusive relationship, so most everyone involved in the case just assumed that he was guilty of her murder. This case unfolds like many episodes of *The Rockford Files*: Rockford uncovers information that leads him to more questions. Rockford finds Lilah's best friend Eunice (Lynn Hamilton), who had faked her own death to start a new life. Eunice informs everyone that Lilah's murder was really a suicide, and that Gandy has two grown children that Eunice had hidden from him.

Under the cover of an in-depth investigation into an unsolved murder, there are several issues presented in "The Hammer of C Block." When Rockford first begins to explore Gandy's case, he goes to Gandy's attorney from twenty years earlier. The attorney says that Gandy's appeal went into the "B and B" file, meaning "black and broke." This is a rare moment on *The Rockford Files* that acknowledges racial differences between the characters, though it does not explore this issue beyond this comment. While the program centers on explorations of class and money, it does not probe questions of race and ethnicity in the same way. It is a constant on the show that Rockford lives on his meager income. However, he does have a safety net in terms of his father, who is always helping Rockford and bailing him out of jail. Gandy does not have that support system, nor does he have the money to pay an attorney to help him appeal his conviction. In a practical sense, both men are not guilty, Gandy because he did not actually pull the trigger to murder Lilah, and Rockford because he was pardoned by the governor. Yet, Rockford is out of prison in five years, and Gandy is left to languish until his term ends and then is forced to reassert his innocence until Rockford intervenes. While Rockford's reintegration into society after prison is not the main focus of the show, episodes such as "The Hammer of C Block" do explore the psychic trauma that is only felt by characters like Rockford and Gandy.

The character Gandy returns for two additional episodes, and in one he wants to become a private detective. The episode "Just Another Polish Wedding" (February 18, 1977) was written as a backdoor pilot episode for Gandy and Marcus Hayes (Louis Gossett Jr.), to establish the men working as private investigators. Over the six seasons of *The Rockford Files* there were several attempts to create characters to spin off into new programs, such as "Just a Coupla Guys" (December 14, 1979), which was discussed in chapter two. Much like "Just a Coupla Guys," the episode's heavy focus is on Hayes and Gandy, largely ignoring Rockford, and was not well received by critics. *Variety*'s

Rockford and Gandy in "The Hammer of C Block."

television critic wrote that the episode was "amusing enough as far as it went—but did not impress as surefire content that would guarantee a steady rating strength if the pilot went to series."[7]

Elder abuse, corruption, and shady real-estate dealings are at the center of the two-part episode "The Trees, the Bees and T. T. Flowers" (Parts 1 and 2, January 21 and 28, 1977). These episodes stand out for several reasons, one of which is that they are told through multiple flashbacks, jumping back to the present time during which Rocky delivers a eulogy at a funeral for an unknown person. The flashback editing allows the episodes to frame a complex story in a way that showcases what proves to be a funeral for a man who is not really dead. The first flashback shows Rocky meeting up with his friend T. T. at his farm. Later, a van from the Horizons Crest Senior Citizen Home arrives and drags T. T. off to be committed. His daughter Cathy and her husband Sherman claim that T. T. is senile, but he is not. Rockford discovers that the doctor at the senior home is drugging people so that they appear to be incoherent and letting family members take on power of attorney to sell off their land. The scheme is connected to corrupt real-estate tycoon Jack Muellard (Scott Brady) and attorney Tom Brockmeyer (Tom Rosqui), all working together to manipulate and defraud senior citizens. Eventually Rockford breaks T. T. out of the senior home, and his daughter soon realizes that her husband Sherman has been manipulating her to get her father's land. The episode wraps up with Rockford's and T. T.'s friends and family watching a news anchor on television make the episode's final point, much like the on-screen text at the end of "So Help Me God." The anchor delivers this news message: "And today, when so many of our mental and convalescent hospitals have become scandal-ridden, one elderly man, Thomas Tyler Flowers, had the courage to stand up for his rights . . . for those who really are in need. How many of these go under, unnoticed, everyday?" This ending monologue sums up the episode and harkens back to how the program works well with this type of episodic social issue—reminding viewers that T. T.'s story is not just about him, but about people everywhere who have been caught up in financial scams.

The season four episode "Trouble in Chapter 17" (September 23, 1977) does what *The Rockford Files* does best—use humor to explore and satirize real-world issues. The character at the center of this episode is Ann Louise Clement (Claudette Nevins), an "anti-feminist" writer who hires Rockford to protect her from her perceived enemies: feminists. When Rockford first meets with her, Ann Louise tells him that the people trying to kill her are "very aggressive, you know. You can't imagine the amount of jealousy and resentment my book has stirred up. And most of them know karate." Rockford listens incredulously and asks, "You don't honestly think the feminist movement is into terrorist activities, do you?" Ann Louise replies, "They are trained revolutionaries, and they want me silenced." Ed Robertson writes that the Clement character is based on Marabel Morgan, a writer who published anti–women's movement books in the 1970s.[8] This character is also likely an amalgam of other anti-feminist activists active in the 1970s, including Phyllis Schlafly, who for many years "traveled the country battling the equal rights amendment."[9] Amid the cultural commentary throughout this episode, it reads as Juanita Bartlett's creative protest against women who built their careers by telling other women that they should not have careers. As noted in the previous chapter, for Bartlett, being a woman writing for television in the 1970s was challenging and uncommon due to the very ideas presented in this episode about "appropriate" careers based on gender.

Aside from the parallels to real-life activists, this episode allows Rockford and Rocky to discuss women and careers. After Rockford says that his client Ann Louise "made two million dollars just saying that the woman's place is in the home," Rocky quickly replies, "It is." Rocky tells Rockford that "they even got ladies pushing rigs," angry about the alleged influx of women into the trucking industry. After Rocky continues to assert his feelings about women working in the home, Rockford tells his father, "It's just a matter of choice, Rocky."

They end the conversation by differently classifying Rocky's attitude: Rocky says he is "old fashioned," and Rockford tells Rocky that he is a "male chauvinist." This exchange between father and son is noteworthy because while the men disagree with one another and are representing two different perspectives about women in the workplace in the 1970s, they do not yell at one another, and both men end the conversation firmly committed to their individual beliefs. However, the program generally frames Rockford as the hero, the person who is able to save others and who has the acumen necessary to solve cases. Rockford's dad, Rocky, is presented as a sweet, caring father, but also as a man of an earlier generation whose ideas about gender roles have become antiquated. So while the writing in the episode allows both Rockford and Rocky's opinions about working women to be voiced, one specific working woman, Rockford's attorney Beth Davenport, consistently saves Rockford from his legal predicaments. Though subtle, Beth's character perhaps serves as a stand-in for Juanita Bartlett or Meta Rosenberg, serving as the one female character in the room with the knowledge to save the men from themselves.

At the heart of this episode are several moments that confront the contradictions of Ann Louise Clement's career. She has built a career on telling women to act in a "traditional" way, but by making her marriage public information, she is also forcing her husband to perform a certain type of masculinity. There are some underlying signals here, that forcing people into rigid roles based on gender serves no one all that well. The ultimate twist of this episode is that everyone involved in the investigation about the attempted murder of Ann Louise had ulterior motives. In the end, Ann Louise's husband Bud (Ed Nelson) leaves her, having grown tired of their relationship being used as material for her books, and it is uncovered that her maid had been doing the housework of a woman whose career it was to tell women to embrace housework.

Juanita Bartlett penned two back-to-back episodes, with "The Battle of Canoga Park" (September 30, 1977) airing the week after

"Trouble in Chapter 17." While these episodes focus on Rockford investigating cases, they also prove to be the gateway that allows the characters to wade into controversial subjects. In "The Battle of Canoga Park," Rockford's gun is stolen and used in a murder, and Lieutenant Diel is convinced that Rockford is guilty of the murder. In an effort to clear his name, Rockford begins investigating and it eventually leads him to a group of people with strong feelings about the constitutional right to bear arms. After tracing a license plate to Lee Ronstadt (Adrienne Marden), Rockford and Dennis Becker go to Ronstadt's house. Ronstadt and her fellow paramilitary group members are concerned enough about their constitutional rights that they have stockpiled weapons and dynamite in the desert. Ronstadt tells the police, "We got a right to bear arms. It's in the Constitution." Rockford says to her, "Well, it's not spelled out in the Constitution, that doesn't mean grenades and bazookas and automatic weapons." As the police are about to detonate the dynamite her group had purchased, Ronstadt says, "We was ready. We was prepared," prompting Rockford to ask her "who were you expecting?" In the next scene Rocky asks the same question as Rockford, and Dennis answers it: "The enemy." Rockford declares them all "certifiable bananas." On several levels this episode is about the U.S. Constitution and the Second Amendment's declaration of the right to bear arms, framing the paramilitary group as having the fringe beliefs about defending themselves from some perceived enemy. Rockford serves as the voice of reason, as a man who owns a gun but tries never to use it. Yet, it is Rockford's gun that is used to murder someone, because he stores it in a too easily accessible space in his trailer: his cookie jar. Overall, the issues raised in "The Battle of Canoga Park" remain as polarizing in the 2020s as they were in the 1970s. Writing for the *Los Angeles Times* in 1975, Paul Houston notes that "most gun control advocates in Congress believe that prospects for strict regulation have not improved significantly," a statement that feels as topical today as it did in 1975.[10] Among the issues explored on *The Rockford Files*, this remains one that continues to resonate in similar ways today.

"The House on Willis Avenue" (February 24, 1978) takes further a thread that appears in many episodes of *The Rockford Files*, covert electronic surveillance and the lack of privacy due to modern technology. In this episode Rockford's friend and fellow private detective Joe Tooley (Paul Fix) has died, apparently in an accident on the freeway. Rockford is immediately suspicious because Tooley did not like driving on the freeway. After his friend's funeral, Rockford goes to Tooley's office to investigate. A man in a room full of computers detects that someone has broken into the office, and he sends two men over to investigate. Rockford soon meets Richie Brockelman (Dennis Dugan), a young private investigator who knows Rockford by reputation. Since Brockelman also suspects something is amiss with Tooley's

Rockford and Dennis investigate a murder in "The Battle of Canoga Park."

death, Rockford begrudgingly agrees to work with him. They go to an office and pretend to be there for equipment repairs. Rockford starts using the computer to look up names and tells Brockelman, "You'd be surprised what you can learn by just punching out a name on one of these control banks. It's spooky," giving a quick sense of Rockford's feelings about new technology and the ease with which it can access private personal information. At many investigative stops, Rockford and Brockelman trigger hidden microphones, suggesting that someone or some group is listening and watching people in many places without their knowledge. With the help of Al Steever (Howard Hesseman), who has been investigating one of the players in this computer scheme, Rockford and Brockelman's investigation eventually leads to Garth McGregor (Jackie Cooper), who is arrested for Tooley's murder. The episode wraps up with Rockford, Brockelman, Rocky, and Steever watching a news report outside Rockford's trailer. On the television the broadcast features a man giving an interview, who tells the group of reporters around him "it appears that Mr. McGregor and the two men who were arrested with him were attempting to set up a secret system of computers which would carry the personal records of some 200 million Americans." The news coverage cuts back to the anchor, who ends the story by noting, "It gives one pause. It's one thing for our government to have us categorized and computerized, but why does a company install a secret underground computer center right in the middle of one of the world's largest cities? Why indeed." Much like the ending postscript on the episode "So Help Me God," a similar statement appears here: "Secret information centers, building dossiers on individuals exist today. You have no legal right to know about them, prevent them, or sue for damages. Our liberty may well be the price we pay for permitting this to continue unchecked. Member, U.S. Privacy Protection Commission." The U.S. Privacy Protection Commission was a real-world organization "created by the Privacy Act of 1974" to study how businesses and institutions were handling "personal information," and then made recommendations to the president and Congress.[11] The commission's findings led to the 1978 Right to Financial Privacy Act, among other legislation, to protect aspects of personal information.[12]

"The House on Willis Avenue" expresses the characters' feelings about covert information gathering through the dialogue noted above, as well as the news report and on-screen text. Again, the program's writers were clearly taking a stance against this intrusive technology that had the capability to spy on unsuspecting people. Of course, its statement must be examined in terms of the episode's negative view of surveillance.[13] Rockford's work is always in service of helping the underdogs of the world, the ones that are being taken advantage of by the rich and the powerful. Here, his unofficial client Tooley has fallen victim to these powerful and dangerous men at the center of this computer surveillance company. Having been caught

Rockford and friends watch the news report about their closed case in "The House on Willis Avenue."

up in a different way in the criminal justice system through his conviction and prison sentence, Rockford's identity has been formed from his firsthand knowledge of the complete lack of privacy in the "panopticon" prison setting, and his desire to prevent this from becoming endemic to life outside of prison. Rockford can help root out corruption but understands that he is essentially powerless to work against people or companies that have the tools and technology to gather information, and the ability to falsify data about people when it serves their needs. At the same time, surveillance and information gathering are central to Rockford's investigative work. The distinction between Rockford's work and the computer here is small but significant. Rockford respects the slow, old-fashioned detective work required of him on most cases, even though it does involve the same tactics as the computer. Rockford's distaste with regard to the technology here is not necessarily that it exists, but in how it can be put to use for nefarious purposes. After all, Rockford himself employs a newer technology at the heart of his private investigative business, his answering machine, a defining feature of his ability to continue working alone.

Though covert surveillance is the central focus of "The House on Willis Avenue," it appears in other episodes as well, such as "The Dog and Pony Show" (October 21, 1977). Rockford's investigation in this episode leads him to a group, the National Intelligence Agency, that is listening in on his client. The episode ends with the realization that someone is now listening to Rockford with hidden microphones, even after his client's case is solved. This pervasive undercurrent of covert surveillance creates self-reflexive moments on the show in which viewers are watching Rockford watch people in his investigations, but the layers of surveillance exist at more levels than even the main characters realize. In another episode, "The Attractive Nuisance" (January 6, 1978), Gretchen Corbett's final appearance on the original run of the show, part of the story involves a man, Bruce Weinstock (Jess Nadelman), who falls off Rockford's trailer and gravely injures himself while planting a listening device. While the bug is not the central story in this episode, this technology does again serve as a reminder to the characters that people are listening, and that the information gathered in this covert and illegal manner continues to put characters in danger.

In total, many episodes of *The Rockford Files* read like a critique of capitalism, and who can and cannot afford to navigate an unjust world. While many of the "bad" players in these episodes are caught and charged with their crimes, they nonetheless repeatedly attempt to take advantage of people for financial gain, through shady real-estate deals or selling access to information gathered through covert surveillance. It is remarkable, and perhaps somewhat unfortunate, that these fifty-year-old television episodes still feel relevant to viewers today. Their continued significance acknowledges how prescient the show's writers were, in terms of recognizing how pervasive and intrusive technology would become in everyday life in the decades after the 1970s, the different interpretations of the Second Amendment, and the fight for justice for victims of crime and those wrongfully accused of crimes. Many of these themes continued to be explored by the writers in the eight made-for-television movies that aired on CBS in the 1990s, which I discuss in the conclusion.

CONCLUSION

"He's Welcomed Back"

The Rockford Files ended its original run in 1980, with a truncated sixth season of eleven episodes.[1] Executive Producer Meta Rosenberg noted at the culmination of the series "it's best to leave when we're still doing good shows."[2] The press reports around the abrupt end to the season suggested that "temperamental star" James Garner was breaking his contract with Universal, and that he had "walked off the job" in the middle of the season.[3] The prior year Garner had shared with Jean Vallely that he was "mentally and physically exhausted" and he had wanted out of the one year remaining in his contract with Universal.[4] In his memoir Garner spoke about how much pain he was in from multiple years of performing his own stunts, and the relentless production schedule of playing the main character in a long-running, hour-long television drama. By the end of *The Rockford Files*, he had undergone "seven knee operations" and was honest about how his acting career had taken a negative toll on his body.[5]

Though he put his body through a lot on *The Rockford Files*, James Garner said he loved making the show. He noted, "When I was making *Rockford* episodes, I used to love to get up and go to work every day," which is why he decided to revisit the character fifteen years later.[6] Well, that and, as he added, "for the money."[7] The original cast, writers, and producers reunited to make eight made-for-television movies that aired between 1994 and 1999 on CBS. Perhaps the most apt metaphor for the stories and the characters that populate *The Rockford Files*, past and present, appears in the first shots of the first reunion movie "I Still Love L.A." (November 27, 1994, also titled "I Love L.A."). A flatbed tow truck drives by with Rockford's Pontiac Firebird with a missing door, broken windows, dents, paint scratches, and missing tires. Viewers would instantly recognize Rockford's signature vehicle, even in its current, less than ideal state. Rockford's car, and the characters reappearing in these reunion films, are back, and while years older with some structural flaws, the essence of their original states remains.

Jim Rockford's Pontiac Firebird in "I Still Love L.A."

These 1990s made-for-television movies revisit many familiar themes from the original series, but they also cover some new ground. In the first reunion movie, "I Still Love L.A.," written by Juanita Bartlett, Rockford is asked to work as an investigator for his friend Kit (Joanna Cassidy), an attorney who is representing Josh (Geoffrey Nauffts) and Dorie (Shannon Kenny), the adult children of her friend Lila Lansing, who has been murdered. Rockford and Kit seem unusually grumpy with one another, and the reason why is revealed through a discussion the characters have at brunch. Rockford says, "What are you having?" and Kit answers, "Flashbacks. Now I remember why I divorced you." Clearly some things have changed, and one of those changes is finally allowing Rockford to settle down, and then to acknowledge that the "settled down life" was not for him. On the other hand, many things in his life in this first movie have not changed much. He is still living in his trailer, though now it is larger and has a small deck. Rockford is still friends with Angel and Dennis. Rockford's relationship with his father is represented by a prominent picture of Rocky on his desk, next to his newer-model answering machine. Noah Beery Jr. was not well enough to appear in this movie and died a few weeks before it aired in late November 1994. The episode is a tribute to him—at the beginning of the credits it reads, "This picture is dedicated to the memory of Noah Beery, Jr. We love you and miss you, Pidge."

What has changed are Rockford's attitude about technology and his choice of clients. As he helps Kit with her case, Rockford observes that the neighbors adjacent to Lansing's mansion have a security camera pointed in the direction where the crime occurred. In several episodes from the 1970s, the characters viewed technology as obtrusive and violating privacy. This technology was presented as being employed for nefarious reasons—such as spying and collecting private personal data. By the 1990s, a security camera used by a private homeowner does not seem as alarming as it had in the past. Again, it is also the show's way of acknowledging how much technology has changed:

Rocky's picture remains on Rockford's desk, alongside his newer answering machine.

from Rockford's old-fashioned investigative techniques to the newer tools employed by private investigators and police officers in the pursuit of solving cases.

Rockford's clients have also changed, somewhat. He was always eager to help a friend, and that person here is Kit. However, Kit is working for two rich twentysomethings who may have murdered their mother, and this disconnect between Rockford's justice-focused worldview brings him into near constant conflict with Kit. So, while Rockford is working for Kit, they are seemingly on different sides, with Kit supporting Lila's adult children, and Rockford defending their former stepfather Mickey Ryder (Joseph Campanella) from allegations that he was a pedophile and a "satanist." While Rockford and Kit realize the truth behind the lies put forth by Josh and Dorie, overall the story does not contain the calming dénouement of an older episode of the show. Without Rocky to re-ground Rockford, it leaves a little tension in the resolution. *The Hollywood Reporter* critic Irv Letofsky reviewed many of the 1990s movies and saw something worthwhile in them. In his review of "I Still Love L.A." Letofsky wrote, "Rockford, still with his sharp eye, still bolder than reason dictates, is one of our endearing heroes, either in new or used episodes. He's welcomed back."[8] What does remain apparent in these reunion movies is the continued examination of money, and how the pursuit of it propels characters to commit illegal or immoral acts.

Juanita Bartlett also wrote "Shoot-out at the Golden Pagoda" (also titled "Murders and Misdemeanors," November 21, 1997), which implicates Rockford in a mess of an investigation that started with fellow private detective and former prison C Block resident Booker Hutch (John Amos). Much like his life-long relationship with Angel, Rockford still gives the people around him multiple opportunities to do the right thing, only to be repeatedly disappointed when they betray him. Likewise, in the Bartlett-penned movie "If the Frame Fits" (January 14, 1996) Rockford is reunited with his old nemeses (with new titles and promotions), Commander Diel and Captain Chapman, who once again assume that Rockford is guilty of murder, and not just the patsy in a frame-up. These episodes revisit Rockford's tendency to trust his friends and people who have been through similar experiences, such as serving time in prison. All three of Bartlett's reunion episodes rely on her adept crafting of multilayered cases that unfold in complex and unexpected ways, slowly revealing the larger crimes and schemes behind the investigations.

Stephen J. Cannell returned to write two of the reunion made-for-television films. In "A Blessing in Disguise" (May 14, 1995), Angel's scheming has led him to some temporary success as a televangelist minister who is staging boycotts against films he deems "blasphemous." Behind the scenes, Rockford discovers that Angel is working with a film production company to concoct these boycotts to boost ticket sales. Much like Cannell's discussions about his father who thought that Cannell was "out of [his] mind . . . trying to be a Hollywood writer," in this movie Rockford serves as a surrogate father to a young actress, Laura Sue Dean (Renée O'Connor), who is the star of the film Angel is working to boycott. Rockford tries to convince Laura Sue that she deserves more from her life and career than a superficial existence in Hollywood. This episode also revisits the changes to investigative work through new and old technology—Rockford is briefly implicated in a murder but is quickly ruled out because Laura Sue photographed the real perpetrators. Again, the underlying issue here is money, and the pursuit of it by manipulating people to act in ways that bring financial gain to the "bad" guys.

Cannell also wrote the script for "Friends and Foul Play" (April 25, 1996). Here, Rockford's friend Babs (Wendy Phillips) wants him to investigate the death of her son, who she believes was murdered. Rockford is initially skeptical about Babs's assessment of her son's death but soon discovers that she was right about her son's murder, but not before Babs and another character are also murdered. Rockford uncovers the underlying motive behind the murders—greed—much like a typical episode of *The Rockford Files*. Rather than a crime family or big corporation, however, the guilty person in this case is a friend of Babs's, Leon (Jason Bernard), a bartender at the restaurant next to Rockford's trailer. Leon had committed these three murders to cover up the fact that he was embezzling money to purchase a yacht and other luxury items.

A third writer from the original series, David Chase, wrote two of the eight CBS made-for-television movies. "Godfather Knows Best" (February 18, 1996) revisits themes expressed throughout Chase's writing on *The Rockford Files*, as well as his later work. Much like Sky Aquarian/Jane Patten/Gopi/Hester in "Quickie Nirvana" (November 11, 1977), this made-for-television movie follows another character who is seeking out meaning in their life—Dennis Becker's son Scotty (Damian Chapa), now homeless at thirty years old and adrift between jobs and school. For a change, instead of Rockford being framed for a murder, Scotty becomes an easy suspect for the murder of a woman who he had allegedly harassed on the street for spare change. In a nod to long-time fans of the show, Rockford brings back one of his old "characters," Jimmy Joe Meeker, now James J. Meeker, who infiltrates a memorial service by masquerading as a health inspector.

While much of *The Rockford Files* showcased the imperfect but loving relationship between Rockford and Rocky, this episode points to a different type of parenting. The Beckers are somewhat implicated as the cause of Scotty's problems—Rockford suggests to Dennis that they had been too lenient, too quickly letting Scotty quit school or his nascent kayaking business. In Scotty's assessment, his father was always more concerned with his work as a police officer than he was with spending time with his son, and this somehow caused him to be a wayward adult. Interestingly, the episode culminates with Scotty finding his way finally, having graduated from the police academy and following his father into this new profession. The subtext here is convoluted—has Scotty really found a new path, or is he just setting himself up to repeat his father's alleged career and family mistakes? Is Scotty going to lose himself in this new career, or is this another attempt to impress his parents by emulating his father's path?

David Chase also wrote and directed "Punishment and Crime" (September 18, 1996), which brought back a recurring character from the original series, Megan Dougherty, played again by Kathryn Harrold. In this return, Megan reveals to Rockford how she really lost her eyesight as a teenager: she was accidentally shot by her cousin Patrick (Bryan Cranston), who has since led a guilt-ridden, troubled life. Both "Godfather Knows Best" and "Punishment and Crime" contain storylines about international crime families that play some part in these murder cases.

The final made-for-television movie feels much like several of the episodes discussed in the previous chapter. "If It Bleeds, It Leads" (April 20, 1999) was written by Reuben Leder, with story by Juanita Bartlett. This last made-for-television movie brings back three-time original series guest star Rita Moreno as Rita Capkovic Landale, now married to Ernie Landale (Hal Linden). In this disturbing episode, Ernie is accused of being a serial rapist because he resembles the sketch of the perpetrator. As a teacher who works with elementary school students, Ernie's career choices are immediately framed negatively, and he is vilified in the press before any actual evidence connects him to these crimes. Even after the rapist is captured, Ernie is not allowed to return to teaching, and he senses that his idyllic life will never be the same. In a scene uncharacteristic of *The Rockford Files*, Ernie dies by suicide by jumping off a high-rise building, in front of Rita, Rockford, Dennis, and the news media gathered at the scene. The ending message here is delivered via a reporter, much like the news anchor in "The Trees, the Bees and T. T. Flowers" (Part 2, January 28, 1977). While the broadcast is live on air, Rockford steps into the camera frame and tells the reporter that their speculative reporting was unconscionable, essentially causing Ernie's death. Unlike earlier episodes in which the news anchor's words linger, or the text onscreen slowly fades to black, the viewer is not given the time to contemplate Rockford's words. Rockford has not even finished his tirade against "the media" when the reporter cuts him off with breaking news about the death of a football player, and the focus immediately shifts away from Rockford and Ernie, who are now demoted to "old" news. In Irv Letofsky's review of the final made-for-television movie, he wrote that it was an "annoying, heavy-fisted polemic against TV news" and that the story was "clumsy and cumbersome."[9] It is also a somber, pessimistic statement about the state of the world in 1999, and a harbinger for things to come, with the show's returning writers treating the subject matter again with the same prescience they had in the original series.

Remakes, Reboots, and Homages

A front-page article in *The Hollywood Reporter* in 2010 states that reboots/remakes of *Hawaii Five-O* and *The Rockford Files* were "so far the most likely pilots to make it to the air in the fall."[10] Writer James Hibberd was correct about the first prediction; *Hawaii Five-O* went on to air for ten seasons on CBS. *The Rockford Files* reboot attached to producer David Shore never came to fruition. Three years later *The Hollywood Reporter* was again reporting on a different reboot of the show, this time with Nic Pizzolatto writing, and with Vince Vaughn stepping into the role as Rockford, for a film rather than a television series.[11] As Mike Fleming Jr. writes, "Universal's sister network NBC tried previously to relaunch this as a TV series, but Vaughn seems like a strong fit for the film."[12] Again, this project failed to move beyond the development stage.

Despite these failed attempts to remake or reboot *The Rockford Files* in the early 2010s, the show's influence continues. There is a little Jim Rockford in the lead characters in several subsequent private detective programs, such as *Monk* (2002–9), *Veronica Mars* (2004–7), *Psych* (2006–14), *Terriers* (2010), and *Poker Face* (2023–), as well as in other genre-bending programs such as *Better Call Saul* (2015–22). Monk (Tony Shalhoub), with his nearly crippling obsessive-compulsive disorder, might be the antithesis of Rockford, but both bring order to the chaos of their investigations, peeling away the evidentiary layers to uncover the truth. On *Veronica Mars*, Veronica (Kristen Bell) is a highly successful private detective who also happens to be a high school (and later, college) student. Though her father Keith Mars (Enrico Colantoni) is also a private detective, much like Rocky he disapproves of Veronica's choice of work and worries incessantly about her safety as she fearlessly investigates dangerous spaces, plays different characters to move her investigations forward, and breaks the law when she deems it necessary.

Psych features detective partners Gus (Dulé Hill) and Shawn (James Roday Rodriguez), the latter of whom pretends to be psychic in order to work on cases with the Santa Barbara Police Department. In reality, Shawn is merely an observant person, like Rockford, who picks up on subtle clues and body language to decipher evidence and solve cases.

In addition to the character similarities, *Psych* finds clever ways to pay homage to its influences. It relies heavily on popular culture references, going so far as to feature stories and casts from existing television shows (such as *Twin Peaks* [1990–91]) to create the homage episode "Dual Spires" (December 1, 2010). *Psych* hints at other influences in smaller ways. For example, in the season two episode "Meat Is Murder, but Murder Is Also Murder" (August 17, 2007), John Amos guest stars as Gus's uncle Burton Guster, ten years after he appeared in "Shoot-out at the Golden Pagoda." Gus's uncle thanks Gus and Shawn for showing him around Santa Barbara for the day, and compares the two men's private detective work to *The Rockford Files*, prompting Shawn to ask Gus "just how much television does he watch?" Of course, everything on the show is a reference to television and other popular culture art forms, deeply self-reflexive, and a wink to fans of the show also familiar with *The Rockford Files*.

Finally, there are notes of many aspects of *The Rockford Files* on *Terriers*, as Ed Robertson notes.[13] The one-season FX program featured two bumbling private detectives, Hank Dolworth (Donal Logue) and Britt Pollack (Michael Raymond-James), who accidentally come across a vast conspiracy with roots across many divisions of a town in California. *Terriers* differs somewhat from *The Rockford Files* in that Rockford's investigations were not accidents; he almost always knew what he was looking for and usually uncovered some truths in his cases. Hank and Britt follow small leads, not knowing that they are going to lead to something much bigger than the original missing person they were seeking.

While *Better Call Saul* is not a detective story per se, nor is Saul/Jimmy (Bob Odenkirk) a detective, his character(s) form a fascinating amalgam of Rockford and Angel: enterprising, resourceful, with a modicum of searching for truth and justice as well. Saul/Jimmy has the tenacity of Rockford and Angel's scoundrel nature, and to borrow Juanita Bartlett's word she always gives Rockford, he's "borderline" between legality and illegality.

The most recent nod toward *The Rockford Files* appears on *Poker Face*, starring Natasha Lyonne as Charlie, a blend of Lieutenant Columbo, Jim Rockford, and perhaps a dabble of Angel Martin as well.[14] In the first episode of the series Charlie wakes up in her trailer, starts her day slowly by visiting with a neighbor and drinking a Coors Light, before being thrust into an investigation around her friend's death and its attempted cover-up by her boss Sterling Frost Jr. (Adrien Brody) and his assistant Cliff (Benjamin Bratt). Charlie has an uncanny ability to read people, then call "bullshit" when someone is lying to her, a gift that is also a curse that forces her to go on the run and work low-profile jobs to keep her off Cliff's radar. Much like many contemporary serialized television programs, Charlie has a "big bad" overarching the series, Sterling Frost Sr. (Ron Perlman), but she also encounters episodic puzzles to solve, or situations to restore, much like episodes of Roy Huggins's pre-*Rockford* program *The Fugitive*, and Stephen J. Cannell's post-*Rockford* program *The A-Team* (1983–87).

An homage to *The Rockford Files*: Charlie's trailer on *Poker Face* in the episode "Dead Man's Hand" (January 26, 2023).

What most of the private detective and genre-bending programs discussed in this chapter have in common with *The Rockford Files* is that they are not "copaganda." That is, they are not programs that are seeking to depict overly positive representations of police officers and police work. They have police officer characters, but they are imperfect, flawed in some ways, and not represented in a largely positive light in the same way they would be on a typical episode of *Law & Order* (1990–2010), *CSI: Crime Scene Investigation* (2000–2015), or *Blue Bloods* (2010–24). Programs like *The Rockford Files* allow for storylines to ask questions of police, policing, and criminal justice without depicting complex institutions as untouchable. This aligns with Horace Newcomb and Paul M. Hirsch's argument in "Television as a Cultural Forum," that examining television allows us "a way of understanding who and what we are, how values and attitudes are adjusted, how meanings shift."[15] In this way, the TV Milestone program *The Rockford Files* truly stands out from other crime-focused programs of the 1970s, asking questions and covering social issues in ways that were not happening elsewhere on television at that time.

It can't be overstated how much *The Rockford Files* has influenced private detective television programs and characters since it first appeared in 1974. It changed the expectations for television private detectives by bringing a new working-class sensibility to the characters by borrowing and remixing the hard-boiled detectives of pulp novels and Hollywood movies. Finally, it never shied away from controversial subject matter, allowing episodes to explore contemporary social issues and broken institutions outside of the framework of the standard police drama. In all, it remains ingrained in the memories of viewers and a frequent topic on social media, both to people who watched it in its original run and those who discovered it long after its initial airing.

The longevity of the show, the love that continues to be poured on these characters, is evidenced in the multiple attempts to reboot/remake the show. The inability to create a new version of *The Rockford*

Files speaks to the unmatchable, perhaps once in a lifetime chemistry between the writers and performers, and the cultural milieu that made the show unique, successful, and pleasurable. In this age of reboots and remakes, it is only a matter of time before a new version of *The Rockford Files* finds its way to television. Hopefully it retains the essence and timeliness of the original.

NOTES

Introduction

1 Elizabeth Withey, "TV Gets Jazzed: The Evolution of Action TV Theme Music," in *Action TV: Tough Guys, Smooth Operators and Foxy Chicks*, ed. Bill Osgerby and Anna Gough-Yates (Routledge, 2001), 202.

2 Jon Abbott, *Stephen J. Cannell Television Productions: A History of All Series and Pilots* (McFarland, 2009), 48.

3 Mark Alvey, "*The Rockford Files*," in *Encyclopedia of Television*, ed. Horace Newcomb (Fitzroy Dearborn, 1997), 1387.

4 Stephen Farber, "Rift Remains After Strike by Writers," *New York Times*, June 30, 1973.

5 Douglas Snauffer, *Crime Television* (Praeger, 2006), 90.

6 Snauffer, *Crime Television*, 91.

7 Snauffer, *Crime Television*, 91.

8 Snauffer, *Crime Television*, 91.

9 David Thorburn, "Detective Programs," in *Encyclopedia of Television*, ed. Horace Newcomb (Fitzroy Dearborn, 1997), 485.

10 Dennis Broe, *Maverick* (Wayne State University Press, 2015), 4.

11 Dahlia Schweitzer, *L.A. Private Eyes* (Rutgers University Press, 2019), 60.

12 Jonathan Nichols-Pethick, *TV Cops: The Contemporary American Television Police Drama* (Routledge, 2012), 2.

13 Roger Sabin et al., *Cop Shows: A Critical History of Police Dramas on Television* (McFarland, 2015), 12.

14 Allen Barra, "Reinventing the American Mystery Story," *New York Times*, September 1, 2002.

15 Alvey, "*The Rockford Files*," 1387.

16 David Marc, *Demographic Vistas: Television in American Culture*, rev. ed. (University of Pennsylvania Press, 1996), 90.

17 Robert F. Gross, "Driving in Circles: *The Rockford Files*," in *Considering David Chase: Essays on "The Rockford Files," "Northern Exposure" and "The Sopranos,"* ed. Thomas Fahy (McFarland, 2008), 31; Abbott, *Stephen J. Cannell Television Productions*, 47.

18 Thorburn, "Detective Programs," 485.

19 Bill Carter, "Stephen J. Cannell, Prolific TV Writer, Dies at 69," *New York Times*, October 2, 2010.

20 Robert Lloyd, "Critic's Notebook: James Garner Was the Perfect Fit in *Rockford Files*," *Los Angeles Times*, July 20, 2014.

21 James Garner and Jon Winokur, *The Garner Files: A Memoir* (Simon & Schuster, 2011), 129.

22 Geoff Tibballs, *Boxtree Encyclopedia of TV Detectives* (Boxtree, 1992), 354.

23 James Garner, interview from *The Rockford Files* season 1, disc 1 DVD bonus feature, Universal Studios Home Entertainment, 2015.

24 Lloyd, "Critic's Notebook: James Garner," 2014.

25 James Lardner, "James Lardner on Television: Rock and Sock," *New Republic*, March 18, 1978, pp. 26–27.

26 Garner and Winokur, *Garner Files*, 131.

27 Snauffer, *Crime Television*, 91.

28 "Noah Beery Jr., 81, an Actor Known for Playing Sidekicks," *New York Times*, November 3, 1994.

29 Richard Meyers, *TV Detectives* (A. S. Barnes, 1981), 212.

30 Alvey, "*The Rockford Files*," 1389.

31 Ed Robertson, *45 Years of "The Rockford Files": An Inside Look at America's Greatest Detective Series*, rev. 3rd ed. (Black Pawn Press, 2020), 8.

32 Jean Vallely, "The James Garner Files," *Esquire*, July 3–19, 1979.

33 Tom Shales, "The Garner Files: Marshmallow Macho," *Washington Post*, May 13, 1979.

34 John Leonard, "The Sitcoms Are Easier to Weather Than the Cop Shows," *New York Times*, November 28, 1976.

35 Abbott, *Stephen J. Cannell Television Productions*, 47.

36 Carter, "Stephen J. Cannell," 2010.

37 Tibballs, *Boxtree Encyclopedia*, 353.

38 Garner, Interview, 2015.

39 Garner and Winokur, *Garner Files*, 128.

40 Gail Williams, "Television Review: *The Rockford Files*," review of *The Rockford Files*, created by Roy Huggins and Stephen J. Cannell, *Hollywood Reporter*, September 28, 1979.

41 James Garner dialogue from "The Kirkoff Case" (September 13, 1974).

42 This movie of the week served as the show's pilot, "Backlash of the Hunter" (March 27, 1974).

43 Bill [Bill Greeley], "Television Review: *The Rockford Files*," review of *The Rockford Files*, created by Roy Huggins and Stephen J. Cannell, *Variety*, September 18, 1974.

44 John J. O'Connor, "TV: *Planet of the Apes*, *Kodiak* and *Chicago and the Man* Bow," *New York Times*, September 13, 1974.

45 Gary Deeb, "Lifting the Lid on the New Season," *Chicago Tribune*, September 8, 1974.

46 "Rhoda Debut Tops National Nielsens," *Los Angeles Times*, September 19, 1974; "NBC Takes the Lead in Nielsen Poll," *Los Angeles Times*, October 25, 1974; "NBC and CBS Vying Closely in Nielsens," *Los Angeles Times*, December 13, 1974.

47 Gary Deeb, "Tempo TV: The News in the 'Rating Game' Is That News Show Flattened the Competition," *Chicago Tribune*, December 10, 1979.

48 Deeb, "Tempo TV: The News in the 'Rating Game,'" 1979.

49 "America's Top Sleuths: A Sleuth Channel Countdown of the Top Sleuths of Television and Film," disc 5, *The Rockford Files* season 4 DVD bonus feature, Universal Studios Home Entertainment, 2015.

50 Amanda D. Lotz, "Must-See TV: NBC's Dominant Decades," in *NBC: America's Network*, ed. Michele Hilmes (University of California Press, 2007), 263.

51 Les Brown, "Where Have All TV Programs Gone? To Fight Ratings War," *New York Times*, January 22, 1977.

52 Robertson, *45 Years of "The Rockford Files,"* 297.

53 Casey Banas, "PTA Rates 'Best,' 'Worst,' on TV," *Chicago Tribune*, February 16, 1978.

54 "The PTA and Television," *Chicago Tribune*, February 17, 1979.

55 Dorothy J. Gaiter, "Lawyer Says 9-Year-Old Bank Robber Was Influenced by TV Crime," *New York Times*, March 2, 1981.

56 I was unable to find specific information about advertisers, which would have added some context to the discussion of viewers and audience.

57 Garner, Interview, 2015.

58 Howard Rosenberg, "Closing the File on Rockford," *Los Angeles Times*, December 7, 1979.

59 Tom Shales, "TV's Violent Departure," *Washington Post*, February 23, 1977.

60 Emily St. James, "In *The Rockford Files*, James Garner Played a PI Who Was in on the Joke," *A.V. Club*, May 2, 2012, https://www.avclub.com/in-the-rockford-files-james-garner-played-a-pi-who-was-1798231199.

61 Miles Beller, "TV Producing—No Longer a Man's World," *New York Times*, July 15, 1979.

62 "The PTA and Television," 1979.

Chapter 1

1 Quote in chapter title from Richard Meyers, *TV Detectives* (A. S. Barnes, 1981), 214.

2 Douglas Snauffer, *Crime Television* (Praeger, 2006), 91.

3 Mark Alvey, "*The Rockford Files*," in *Encyclopedia of Television*, ed. Horace Newcomb (Fitzroy Dearborn, 1997), 1389.

4 James Garner, interview from *The Rockford Files* season 1, disc 1 DVD bonus feature, Universal Studios Home Entertainment, 2015.

5 Meyers, *TV Detectives*, 214.

6 James Garner and Jon Winokur, *The Garner Files: A Memoir* (Simon & Schuster, 2011), 130.

7 Snauffer, *Crime Television*, 91.

8 This episode originally aired on October 18, 1974. On the *Rockford Files* DVD set this episode was split up into two episodes, Parts I and II. Rocky's quote here is from Part II.

9 Ed Robertson, *45 Years of "The Rockford Files": An Inside Look at America's Greatest Detective Series*, rev. 3rd ed. (Black Pawn Press, 2020), 68.

10 Alvey, "*The Rockford Files*," 1389.

11 Robertson, *45 Years of "The Rockford Files,"* 300.

12 Diel's name is sometimes spelled Diehl. In the episode "The Countess" (September 27, 1974) you can see his name on his office door, Lt. Alex Diel,

at 23:30. However, in the episode "The Battle of Canoga Park" (September 30, 1977) it is spelled Diehl on his door. For the sake of consistency, I spell it Diel throughout this book.

13 James Lardner, "James Lardner on Television: Rock and Sock," *New Republic*, March 18, 1978, pp. 26–27.

14 Meyers, *TV Detectives*, 212.

15 Garner and Winokur, *Garner Files*, 130.

16 Alvey, "*The Rockford Files*," 1389.

Chapter 2

1 Quote in chapter title from Ed Robertson, *45 Years of "The Rockford Files": An Inside Look at America's Greatest Detective Series*, rev. 3rd ed. (Black Pawn Press, 2020), 19.

2 Miles Beller, "TV Producing—No Longer a Man's World," *New York Times*, July 15, 1979.

3 Jennifer Keishin Armstrong, *When Women Invented Television: The Untold Story of the Female Powerhouses Who Pioneered the Way We Watch Today* (HarperCollins, 2021), xiv.

4 Muriel Davidson, "James Garner: A Really Nice Guy Makes Good," *Good Housekeeping*, March 1976.

5 Davidson, "James Garner," 1976.

6 Dennis Broe, *Maverick* (Wayne State University Press, 2015), 114n9.

7 Douglas Snauffer, *Crime Television* (Praeger, 2006), 91.

8 Robert J. Thompson, *Adventures on Prime Time: The Television Programs of Stephen J. Cannell* (Praeger, 1990), 54.

9 Bill Carter, "Stephen J. Cannell, Prolific TV Writer, Dies at 69," *New York Times*, October 2, 2010.

10 Carter, "Stephen J. Cannell," 2010.

11 Tom Shales, "The Garner Files: Marshmallow Macho," *Washington Post*, May 13, 1979. I can't find an exact date that Rosenberg began working as Garner's agent, but most accounts say "around 1960." See Mollie Gregory, *Women Who Run the Show: How a Brilliant and Creative New Generation of Women Stormed Hollywood* (St. Martin's Press, 2002), 103.

12 Gregory, *Women Who Run the Show*, 103.

13 Robertson, *45 Years of "The Rockford Files,"* 16.

14 Myrna Oliver, "Meta Rosenberg, 89: Agent, *Rockford Files* Producer," *Los Angeles Times*, January 11, 2005.

15 Oliver, "Meta Rosenberg," 2005.

16 Oliver, "Meta Rosenberg," 2005.

17 Victor S. Navasky, *Naming Names* (Viking Press, 1980), 141, 174. See also Robert Vaughn, *Only Victims: A Study of Show Business Blacklisting* (G. P. Putnam's Sons, 1972).

18 Gregory, *Women Who Run the Show*, 103.

19 Meta Rosenberg, "Meta Rosenberg: Agent/Producer," interview by Sunny Parich, *Television Academy*, February 12, 1998, https://interviews.televisionacademy.com/interviews/meta-rosenberg.

20 Robertson, *45 Years of "The Rockford Files,"* 53; there were other women writers employed by the show, including Gloryette Clark and Leigh Brackett, and two women with "story by" credits, Dorothy J. Bailey and Maryann Rea.

21 Robertson, *45 Years of "The Rockford Files,"* 53.

22 Robertson, *45 Years of "The Rockford Files,"* 53.

23 James Garner and Jon Winokur, *The Garner Files: A Memoir* (Simon & Schuster, 2011), 124.

24 Garner and Winokur, *Garner Files*, 213.

25 Robertson, *45 Years of "The Rockford Files,"* 285.

26 Kendall R. Phillips, *Kolchak: The Night Stalker* (Wayne State University Press, 2022).

27 Rosenberg, "Meta Rosenberg: Agent/Producer," 1998.

28 Victoria E. Johnson, "From Paradise Cove to the Precinct: Mapping *The Rockford Files*' Urban (Tele)Visions," in *Considering David Chase: Essays on "The Rockford Files," "Northern Exposure" and "The Sopranos,"* ed. Thomas Fahy (McFarland, 2008), 22–23.

29 Of the other three directed episodes, two were written by Stephen J. Cannell and one by Juanita Bartlett.

30 Mick [Larry Michie], "TV Followup," *Variety*, December 19, 1979.

31 Michael E. Hill, "Charles Johnson," *Washington Post*, May 1, 1988.

32 Charles Floyd Johnson, "Foundation Interviews: Charles Floyd Johnson," interview by Adrienne Faillace, *Television Academy*, February 13, 2023, https://www.emmys.com/news/interviews-archive/charles-floyd-johnson.

33 Garner and Winokur, *Garner Files*, 124.

34 Robertson, *45 Years of "The Rockford Files,"* 35.

35 Robertson, *45 Years of "The Rockford Files,"* 36.

Chapter 3

1 "For Your Emmy Consideration . . . *The Rockford Files*," *Hollywood Reporter*, July 28, 1978.

2 James Lardner, "James Lardner on Television: Rock and Sock," *New Republic*, March 18, 1978, pp. 26–27.

3 Howard Rosenberg, "Closing the File on Rockford," *Los Angeles Times*, December 7, 1979.

4 James Garner and Jon Winokur, *The Garner Files: A Memoir* (Simon & Schuster, 2011), 124.

5 For a journalistic account about land fraud in the 1970s, see Grace Lichtenstein, "Arizona and New Mexico Striving to Combat Fraud in Land Sales," *New York Times*, September 13, 1976.

6 Warren Weaver Jr., "Bar Group Urges Help for Grand Jury Witnesses," *New York Times*, August 10, 1977. See also Leslie Maitland, "Gigante Won't Waive Immunity in Inquiry," *New York Times*, September 8, 1977.

7 Bok [Bob Knight], "TV Followups: *The Rockford Files*," review of *The Rockford Files*, created by Roy Huggins and Stephen J. Cannell, *Variety*, February 23, 1977.

8 Ed Robertson, *45 Years of "The Rockford Files": An Inside Look at America's Greatest Detective Series*, rev. 3rd ed. (Black Pawn Press, 2020), 254.

9 Ginia Bellafante, "At Home with Phyllis Schlafly: A Feminine Mystique All Her Own," *New York Times*, March 30, 2006.

10 Paul Houston, "Chances of Gun Curbs Still Seem Slim," *Los Angeles Times*, September 30, 1975. See also Paul Houston, "Gun Lobby Seeks Millions to Fight Its Foes at Polls," *Los Angeles Times*, April 25, 1976.

11 David F. Linowes, "The U.S. Privacy Protection Commission: A Retrospective View from the Chair," *American Behavior Scientists* 26, no. 5 (May/June 1983): 577.

12 Linowes, "The U.S. Privacy Protection Commission," 587.

13 For journalistic coverage of issues around surveillance in the 1970s, see Nicholas M. Horrock, "President Limits U.S. Surveillance of Citizens' Lives," *New York Times*, February 19, 1976; Warren Weaver Jr., "Justices Relax Rule on Phones in Surveillance," *New York Times*, December 8, 1977.

Conclusion

1 Quote in chapter title from Irv Letofsky, "TV Review: *The Rockford Files*," review of *The Rockford Files*, created by Roy Huggins and Stephen J. Cannell, *Hollywood Reporter*, November 23, 1994.

2 Howard Rosenberg, "Closing the File on Rockford," *Los Angeles Times*, December 7, 1979.

3 Gary Deeb, "Tempo TV: Garner and Klugman Vanish at a Prime Time," *Chicago Tribune*, January 2, 1980.

4 Jean Vallely, "The James Garner Files," *Esquire*, July 3–19, 1979.

5 James Garner and Jon Winokur, *The Garner Files: A Memoir* (Simon & Schuster, 2011), 134.

6 Garner and Winokur, *Garner Files*, 143.

7 Garner and Winokur, *Garner Files*, 143.

8 Letofsky, "TV Review: *The Rockford Files*," 1994.

9 Irv Letofsky, "TV Review: *The Rockford Files*; If It Bleeds . . . It Leads," review of *The Rockford Files*, created by Roy Huggins and Stephen J. Cannell, *Hollywood Reporter*, April 19, 1999.

10 James Hibberd, "Some Pilots Take Off Faster Than Others," *Hollywood Reporter*, April 26, 2010.

11 Borys Kit, "*Rockford Files* Enlists Hot Writer," *Hollywood Reporter*, November 8, 2013.

12 Mike Fleming Jr., "Chuck Hogan on the Case for Vince Vaughn and *The Rockford Files*," *Deadline*, April 4, 2014, https://deadline.com/2014/04/chuck-hogan-on-the-case-for-vince-vaughn-and-the-rockford-files-709427/.

13 Ed Robertson, *45 Years of "The Rockford Files": An Inside Look at America's Greatest Detective Series*, rev. 3rd ed. (Black Pawn Press, 2020), 434.

14 See Amanda Keeler, "You Have to Watch It! You Love *Columbo*: Prestige Television and *Poker Face*," *Velvet Light Trap* 93 (2024).

15 Horace Newcomb and Paul M. Hirsch, "Television as a Cultural Forum," in *Television: The Critical View*, 6th ed., ed. Horace Newcomb (Oxford University Press, 2000), 564.

WORKS CITED

Abbott, Jon. *Stephen J. Cannell Television Productions: A History of All Series and Pilots.* McFarland, 2009.

Alvey, Mark. "*The Rockford Files.*" In *Encyclopedia of Television*, edited by Horace Newcomb. Fitzroy Dearborn, 1997.

"America's Top Sleuths: A Sleuth Channel Countdown of the Top Sleuths of Television and Film." Disc 5. *The Rockford Files*, season 4 DVD bonus feature. Universal Studios Home Entertainment, 2015.

Armstrong, Jennifer Keishin. *When Women Invented Television: The Untold Story of the Female Powerhouses Who Pioneered the Way We Watch Today.* Harper-Collins, 2021.

Banas, Casey. "PTA Rates 'Best,' 'Worst,' on TV." *Chicago Tribune*, February 16, 1978.

Barra, Allen. "Reinventing the American Mystery Story." *New York Times*, September 1, 2002.

Bellafante, Ginia. "At Home with Phyllis Schlafly: A Feminine Mystique All Her Own." *New York Times*, March 20, 2006.

Beller, Miles. "TV Producing—No Longer a Man's World." *New York Times*, July 15, 1979.

Bill [Bill Greeley]. "Television Review: *The Rockford Files.*" Review of *The Rockford Files*, created by Roy Huggins and Stephen J. Cannell. *Variety*, September 18, 1974.

Bok [Bob Knight]. "TV Followups: *The Rockford Files.*" Review of *The Rockford Files*, created by Roy Huggins and Stephen J. Cannell. *Variety*, February 23, 1977.

Broe, Dennis. *Maverick*. Wayne State University Press, 2015.

Brown, Les. "Where Have All TV Programs Gone? To Fight Ratings War." *New York Times*, January 22, 1977.

Carter, Bill. "Stephen J. Cannell, Prolific TV Writer, Dies at 69." *New York Times*, October 2, 2010.

Chicago Tribune. "The PTA and Television." February 17, 1979.

Davidson, Muriel. "James Garner: A Really Nice Guy Makes Good." *Good Housekeeping*, March 1976.

Deeb, Gary. "Lifting the Lid on the New Season." *Chicago Tribune*, September 8, 1974.

Deeb, Gary. "Tempo TV: Garner and Klugman Vanish at a Prime Time." *Chicago Tribune*, January 2, 1980.

Deeb, Gary. "Tempo TV: The News in the 'Rating Game' Is That News Show Flattened the Competition." *Chicago Tribune*, December 10, 1979.

Farber, Stephen. "Rift Remains After Strike by Writers." *New York Times*, June 30, 1973.

Fleming, Mike, Jr. "Chuck Hogan on the Case for Vince Vaughn and *The Rockford Files*." *Deadline*, April 4, 2014. https://deadline.com/2014/04/chuck-hogan-on-the-case-for-vince-vaughn-and-the-rockford-files-709427/.

Gaiter, Dorothy J. "Lawyer Says 9-Year-Old Bank Robber Was Influenced by TV Crime." *New York Times*, March 2, 1981.

Garner, James. Interview from *The Rockford Files* season 1, disc 1 DVD bonus feature. Universal Studios Home Entertainment, 2015.

Garner, James, and Jon Winokur. *The Garner Files: A Memoir*. Simon & Schuster, 2011.

Green, Paul. *Roy Huggins: Creator of "Maverick," "77 Sunset Strip," "The Fugitive" and "The Rockford Files."* McFarland, 2014.

Gregory, Mollie. *Women Who Run the Show: How a Brilliant and Creative New Generation of Women Stormed Hollywood*. St. Martin's Press, 2002.

Gross, Robert F. "Driving in Circles: *The Rockford Files*." In *Considering David Chase: Essays on "The Rockford Files," "Northern Exposure" and "The Sopranos,"* edited by Thomas Fahy. McFarland, 2008.

Hibberd, James. "Some Pilots Take Off Faster Than Others." *Hollywood Reporter*, April 26, 2010.

Hill, Michael E. "Charles Johnson." *Washington Post*, May 1, 1988.

Hollywood Reporter. "For Your Emmy Consideration . . . *The Rockford Files*." July 28, 1978.

Horrock, Nicholas M. "President Limits U.S. Surveillance of Citizens' Lives." *New York Times*, February 19, 1976.

Houston, Paul. "Chances of Gun Curbs Still Seem Slim." *Los Angeles Times*, September 30, 1975.

Houston, Paul. "Gun Lobby Seeks Millions to Fight Its Foes at Polls." *Los Angeles Times*, April 25, 1976.

Johnson, Charles Floyd. "Foundation Interviews: Charles Floyd Johnson." Interview by Adrienne Faillace. *Television Academy*, February 13, 2023. https://www.emmys.com/news/interviews-archive/charles-floyd-johnson.

Johnson, Victoria E. "From Paradise Cove to the Precinct: Mapping *The Rockford Files*' Urban (Tele)Visions." In *Considering David Chase: Essays on "The Rockford Files," "Northern Exposure" and "The Sopranos,"* edited by Thomas Fahy. McFarland, 2008.

Keeler, Amanda. "You Have to Watch It! You Love *Columbo*: Prestige Television and *Poker Face*." *Velvet Light Trap* 93 (2024): 55–56.

Kit, Borys. "*Rockford Files* Enlists Hot Writer." *Hollywood Reporter*, November 8, 2013.

Lardner, James. "James Lardner on Television: Rock and Sock." *New Republic*, March 18, 1978.

Leonard, John. "The Sitcoms Are Easier to Weather Than the Cop Shows." *New York Times*, November 28, 1976.

Letofsky, Irv. "TV Review: *The Rockford Files*." Review of *The Rockford Files*, created by Roy Huggins and Stephen J. Cannell. *Hollywood Reporter*, November 23, 1994.

Letofsky, Irv. "TV Review: *The Rockford Files*; If It Bleeds . . . It Leads." Review of *The Rockford Files*, created by Roy Huggins and Stephen J. Cannell. *Hollywood Reporter*, April 19, 1999.

Lichtenstein, Grace. "Arizona and New Mexico Striving to Combat Fraud in Land Sales." *New York Times*, September 13, 1976.

Linowes, David F. "The U.S. Privacy Protection Commission: A Retrospective View from the Chair." *American Behavior Scientists* 26, no. 5 (May/June 1983): 577–90.

Lloyd, Robert. "Critic's Notebook: James Garner Was the Perfect Fit in *Rockford Files*." *Los Angeles Times*, July 20, 2014.

Los Angeles Times. "NBC and CBS Vying Closely in Nielsens." December 13, 1974.

Los Angeles Times. "NBC Takes the Lead in Nielsen Poll." October 25, 1974.

Los Angeles Times. "Rhoda Debut Tops National Nielsens." September 19, 1974.

Lotz, Amanda D. "Must-See TV: NBC's Dominant Decades." In *NBC: America's Network*, edited by Michele Hilmes. University of California Press, 2007.

Maitland, Leslie. "Gigante Won't Waive Immunity in Inquiry." *New York Times*, September 8, 1977.

Marc, David. *Demographic Vistas: Television in American Culture*. Rev. ed. University of Pennsylvania Press, 1996.

Meyers, Richard. *TV Detectives*. A. S. Barnes, 1981.

Mick [Larry Michie]. "TV Followup." *Variety*, December 19, 1979.

Navasky, Victor S. *Naming Names*. Viking Press, 1980.

New York Times. "Noah Beery Jr., 81, an Actor Known for Playing Sidekicks." November 3, 1994.

Newcomb, Horace, and Paul M. Hirsch. "Television as a Cultural Forum." In *Television: The Critical View*, 6th ed., edited by Horace Newcomb. Oxford University Press, 2000.

Nichols-Pethick, Jonathan. *TV Cops: The Contemporary American Television Police Drama*. Routledge, 2012.

O'Connor, John J. "TV: *Planet of the Apes*, *Kodiak* and *Chicago and the Man* Bow." *New York Times*, September 13, 1974.

Oliver, Myrna. "Meta Rosenberg, 89: Agent, *Rockford Files* Producer." *Los Angeles Times*, January 11, 2005.

Phillips, Kendall R. *Kolchak: The Night Stalker*. Wayne State University Press, 2022.

Robertson, Ed. *45 Years of "The Rockford Files": An Inside Look at America's Greatest Detective Series*. Rev. 3rd ed. Black Pawn Press, 2020.

Rosenberg, Howard. "Closing the File on Rockford." *Los Angeles Times*, December 7, 1979.

Rosenberg, Meta. "Meta Rosenberg: Agent/Producer." Interview by Sunny Parich. *Television Academy*, February 12, 1998. https://interviews.televisionacademy.com/interviews/meta-rosenberg.

Sabin, Roger, Ronald Wilson, Linda Speidel, Brian Faucette, and Ben Bethell. *Cop Shows: A Critical History of Police Dramas on Television*. McFarland, 2015.

Schweitzer, Dahlia. *L.A. Private Eyes*. Rutgers University Press, 2019.

Shales, Tom. "The Garner Files: Marshmallow Macho." *Washington Post*, May 13, 1979.

Shales, Tom. "TV's Violent Departure." *Washington Post*, February 23, 1977.

Snauffer, Douglas. *Crime Television*. Praeger, 2006.

St. James, Emily. "In *The Rockford Files*, James Garner Played a PI Who Was in on the Joke." *A.V. Club*, May 2, 2012. https://www.avclub.com/in-the-rockford-files-james-garner-played-a-pi-who-was-1798231199.

Thompson, Robert J. *Adventures on Prime Time: The Television Programs of Stephen J. Cannell*. Praeger, 1990.

Thorburn, David. "Detective Programs." In *Encyclopedia of Television*, edited by Horace Newcomb. Fitzroy Dearborn, 1997.

Tibballs, Geoff. *Boxtree Encyclopedia of TV Detectives*. Boxtree, 1992.

Vallely, Jean. "The James Garner Files." *Esquire*, July 3–19, 1979.

Vaughn, Robert. *Only Victims: A Study of Show Business Blacklisting*. G. P. Putnam's Sons, 1972.

Weaver, Warren, Jr. "Bar Group Urges Help for Grand Jury Witnesses." *New York Times*, August 10, 1977.

Weaver, Warren, Jr. "Justices Relax Rule on Phones in Surveillance." *New York Times*, December 8, 1977.

Williams, Gail. "Television Review: *The Rockford Files*." Review of *The Rockford Files*, created by Roy Huggins and Stephen J. Cannell. *Hollywood Reporter*, September 28, 1979.

Withey, Elizabeth. "TV Gets Jazzed: The Evolution of Action TV Theme Music." In *Action TV: Tough Guys, Smooth Operators and Foxy Chicks*, edited by Bill Osgerby and Anna Gough-Yates. Routledge, 2001.

INDEX

Abbott, Jon, 3, 13
Alvey, Mark, 6, 21, 32
Amos, John, 85, 90
anti-feminist activism, 73–74
arms, right to bear, 75–76
Armstrong, Jennifer Keishin, 43

Bailey, Dorothy J., 100n20
Barra, Allen, 6
Bartlett, Juanita, 50–57; accolades for, 17; and anti-feminist activism, 73; episodes written by, 36, 62–63, 74–75; and made-for-television movies, 85, 87–88; and social issues addressed in *The Rockford Files*, 65–69; and women in television, 43
Becker, Dennis (character), 10, 22, 33–36
Beery, Noah, Jr., 22, 23, 83. *See also* Rockford, Joseph "Rocky" (character)
Better Call Saul (2015–22), 90
Brackett, Leigh, 100n20
Broe, Dennis, 44
Brown, Les, 17

Cannell, Stephen J., 44–46; and Charles Johnson, 63; and creation of *The Rockford Files*, 3–4, 11, 21; on Jim Rockford's family, 22–23; made-for-television movies written by, 85–86; and social issues addressed in *The Rockford Files*, 65; and success of *The Rockford Files*, 43; on violence in *The Rockford Files*, 18
Capkovic, Rita (character), 55–57
Carpenter, Pete, 2
Carter, Bill, 7, 13, 17
characters, 21–22; Angel Martin, 22, 37–41; Beth Davenport, 22, 27–33, 74; Dennis Becker, 10, 22, 33–36; Jim Rockford, 1–2, 4, 6–13, 73–74; Rocky Rockford, 11, 22–27, 73–74
Chase, David, 44, 46–47, 57–61, 63, 86–87

Clark, Gloryette, 100n20
Clement, Ann Louise (character), 73, 74
Communist Party, 47
"copaganda," 92
Corbett, Gretchen, 27–28, 33. *See also* Davenport, Beth (character)
corruption, 72, 79
criminal justice system, 38, 67–69, 78–79

Davenport, Beth (character), 22, 27–33, 74. *See also* Corbett, Gretchen
Davidson, Muriel, 43
Deeb, Gary, 16
Donley, Robert, 23
Dougherty, Megan (character), 60, 87

elder abuse, 72–73
electronic surveillance, 76–80, 83–84
episodes: "The Aaron Ironwood School of Success," 24–26; "The Attractive Nuisance," 79–80; "Backlash of the Hunter," 38, 66; "The Battle of Canoga Park," 74–75; "The Becker Connection," 36, 63; "Black Mirror," 60; "Chicken Little Is a Little Chicken," 39; "Coulter City Wildcat," 62; "The Countess," 34–35, 62; "Crack Back," 30–31; "The Dark and Bloody Ground," 28–29, 33–34; "A Deadly Maze," 55; "Deep Blue Sleep," 63; "The Dog and Pony Show," 58–59, 79; "The Farnsworth Stratagem," 35–36, 52, 53, 56, 69; "Find Me If You Can," 35; "Forced Retirement," 31–32; "Foul on the First Play," 63; "The Four Pound Brick," 26; "The Fourth Man," 55; "The Girl in the Bay City Boys Club," 53–55; "A Good Clean Bust with Sequel Rights," 26; "The Great Blue Lake Land and Development Company," 51, 66–67; "The Hammer of C Block," 69–71; "The Hawaiian Headache," 27; "Heartaches of a Fool," 45–46; "The House on Willis Avenue," 76–79; "Just a Coupla Guys," 61, 71; "Just Another Polish Wedding," 71–72; "The Kirkoff Case," 13–16; "Love Is the Word," 60; "No Fault Affair," 27, 56–57; "The Paper Palace," 56; "Piece Work," 55; "A Portrait of Elizabeth," 29–30, 48; "The Prisoner of Rosemont Hall," 63; "Quickie Nirvana," 59, 86; "Rattlers' Class of '63," 39–41, 48–49; "Resurrection in Black & White," 53; "Rosendahl and Gilda Stern Are Dead," 56; "So Help Me God," 51, 66, 67–69; "There's One in Every Port," 49–50, 69; "The Trees, the Bees and T. T. Flowers," 26–27, 72–73, 88; "Trouble in Chapter 17," 73–74; "White on White and Nearly Perfect," 44–45. *See also* made-for-television movies

female "helpers," 51–53, 54–55, 59
feminism, 73–74
Fifth Amendment, 67
Fitch, Gandolph "Gandy" (character), 70–72
flashback editing, 72
Fleming, Mike, Jr., 89

Garner, James: accolades for, 16–17; acting experience of, 12; on

casting of Stuart Margolin, 38; on characters, 21; on Charles Johnson, 62; chemistry with other actors, 22, 23; comedic talent of, 12; and end of *The Rockford Files*, 81; episode directed by, 53–55; on Jim Rockford, 8, 9; on Juanita Bartlett, 51; on making *Rockford* episodes, 81–82; portrayal of Jim Rockford, 11–13; on Rockford's relationship with police, 10; support for women, 43; on violence in *The Rockford Files*, 18. *See also* Rockford, Jim (character)
grand jury system, 67–69
Greeley, Bill, 15–16
Gregory, Mollie, 46, 47
gun control, 75–76

Harrold, Kathryn, 60, 87
Hawaii Five-O, 88–89
heart-to-heart conversations, 48–50, 59–60
"helpers," female, 51–53, 54–55, 59
Hibberd, James, 89
Hill, Michael E., 61–62
Hirsch, Paul M., 92
homages, 89–93
House Un-American Activities Committee (HUAC), 47
Houston, Paul, 75
Huggins, Roy, 3–4, 43, 50–51

Johnson, Charles Floyd, 44, 61–63
Johnson, Victoria E., 58
justice, 10

Lardner, James, 10, 37, 65
Leder, Reuben, 87–88
Leonard, John, 12
Letofsky, Irv, 85, 88
Lloyd, Robert, 10
Lotz, Amanda D., 17

made-for-television movies: "A Blessing in Disguise," 85–86; "Friends and Foul Play," 86; "Godfather Knows Best," 61, 86–87; "If It Bleeds, It Leads," 87–88; "If the Frame Fits," 85; "I Still Love L.A." ("I Love L.A."), 82–85; "Punishment and Crime," 87; "Shoot-out at the Golden Pagoda" ("Murders and Misdemeanors"), 85
Mannix (1967–75), 4
Marc, David, 6
Margolin, Stuart, 17, 37–38. *See also* Martin, Angel (character)
Martin, Angel (character), 22, 37–41. *See also* Margolin, Stuart
Meyers, Richard, 11, 38
Michie, Larry (Mick), 61
Mick (Larry Michie), 61
Monk (2002–9), 89
Moreno, Rita, 55–57, 88
Morgan, Marabel, 73

Newcomb, Horace, 92
Nichols-Pethick, Jonathan, 5

O'Connor, John J., 16

Parent Teacher Association (PTA), 17–18
Pizzolatto, Nic, 89
Poker Face (2023–), 91
Post, Mike, 2, 17
post-prison life, 69–71

privacy, 83–84
Psych (2006–14), 89–90

Rea, Maryann, 100n20
real-estate fraud, 66–67, 72
remakes/reboots, 88–89, 92–93
Robertson, Ed, 12, 17, 46, 51, 73, 90
Rockford, Jim (character): character and personality of, 1–2, 4, 6–13; as feminist, 73–74. *See also* Garner, James
Rockford, Joseph "Rocky" (character), 2, 11, 22–27, 73–74. *See also* Beery, Noah, Jr.
Rockford Files, The: accolades for, 16–17, 58; conception and creation of, 3–4; criticism of, 17–18; end of, 81; genre of, 4–6; influence of, 92; made-for-television movies, 82–88; ratings for, 16, 17; remakes, reboots, and homages to, 88–93; series premiere of, 13–16; social issues tackled by, 65–80; success of, 43; theme song, 2–3; tone of, 12; as TV Milestone, 3. *See also* characters; episodes
Rosenberg, Howard, 65
Rosenberg, Meta, 43, 46–50, 58, 59, 81

Sabin, Roger, 5
Schlafly, Phyllis, 73
Schweitzer, Dahlia, 5
Second Amendment, 75–76
Shales, Tom, 12
Shore, David, 89
60 Minutes, 66–67
social class, 68–69, 70
social issues, 65–80
surveillance, electronic, 76–80, 83–84

technology, 76–80, 83–84
Terriers (2010), 90
theme song, 2–3
Thorburn, David, 5, 7
Tibballs, Geoff, 8–9

U.S. Privacy Protection Commission, 77–78

Vallely, Jean, 12, 81
Vaughn, Vince, 89
Veronica Mars (2004–7), 89
violence, 17–18

Weaver, Warren, Jr., 69
Williams, Gail, 13
women: female "helpers," 51–53, 54–55, 59; and feminist debates, 73–74; in television, 43. *See also* Bartlett, Juanita; Rosenberg, Meta